"I'd threaten you with a sexual harassment lawsuit but you flirt with everyone at the bar except me. Why is that?"

"You're the one pressed up against me." He shifted, somehow drawing her closer without pulling her to him. "Who's doing the harassing?"

He was right, but she could sense that his need matched her own. In the quiet intimacy of her apartment, it made her bold enough to ask, "Does this feel like harassment, Scott?"

"This feels like heaven," he whispered. "But I didn't come here for this. I'm no good for you."

"That's the point. I'm looking for a wild adventure and developing a new fondness for things that aren't good for me."

He took her arms and lifted them around his neck. Her head tilted and he brushed his lips against hers. Finally. It felt like she'd been waiting for this kiss her entire life.

And it was worth it.

Dear Reader,

I love the word *home* and the emotions it conjures. It's the place you hang your hat or where you find solace at the end of a long day. The people and the love you find at home also make it so special.

After an impulsive decision leaves attorney Lexi Preston without a home, she comes to Brevia, North Carolina, looking for a fresh start. Something about this small mountain town gives her hope that with a new beginning, she can change her life for the better.

Scott Callahan isn't sure what to make of Lexi and her endless optimism. Resigned to his loner's life, Scott is reluctant to make amends with his family. And he certainly won't admit that he yearns for a place to call home as much as Lexi does.

Lexi and Scott are a classic case of opposites attract. But if they realize just how perfect they are for each other, these two might find their forever love in *A Brevia Beginning*.

I'm happy you picked up this book and would love to hear from you. Visit my website at www.michellemajor.com or email me at michelle@michellemajor.com.

All the best,

Michelle Major

A Brevia Beginning

Michelle Major

HARLEQUIN® SPECIAL EDITION®

Recycling programs
for this product may
not exist in your area.

ISBN-13: 978-0-373-65822-0

A BREVIA BEGINNING

Copyright © 2014 by Michelle Major

This edition published by arrangement with Harlequin Books S.A.

For questions and comments about the quality of this book, please contact us
at CustomerService@Harlequin.com.

® and TM are trademarks of Harlequin Enterprises Limited or its corporate
affiliates. Trademarks indicated with ® are registered in the United States Patent
and Trademark Office, the Canadian Trade Marks Office and in other countries.

Printed in U.S.A.

Books by Michelle Major

Harlequin Special Edition

Still the One #2244
Her Accidental Engagement #2321
A Brevia Beginning #2340

Other titles by this author available in ebook format.

MICHELLE MAJOR

grew up in Ohio, but dreamed of living in the mountains. Soon after graduating with a degree in journalism, she pointed her car west and settled in Colorado. Her life and house are filled with one great husband, two beautiful kids, a few furry pets and several well-behaved reptiles. She's grateful to have found her passion writing stories with happy endings. Michelle loves to hear from her readers at www.michellemajor.com.

To my grandmother, Ruth Keller,
for believing in me and my writing
from the time I was a little girl. I love you, Gram.

Chapter One

The street was deserted in the early-morning hours. Sunlight slanted over the roofs of the brick buildings as Lexi Preston huddled on the front stoop of a dark storefront. She rested her head in her hands and watched the wind swirl a small pile of autumn leaves. The air held a chill, but it felt good after being stuck in her car for the last day and a half.

Almost six months had passed since she'd set foot in Brevia, North Carolina. She couldn't imagine the reception she'd receive, but was desperate enough not to care. Her eyes drifted shut—just for a minute, she told herself—but she must have fallen asleep. When she blinked them open again it was to the bright sun shining and someone nudging a foot against hers. She scrambled to her feet, embarrassed to be caught so off guard.

"What the hell do you want?" Julia Callahan's voice cut through the quiet.

Lexi backed away a few steps. Yes, she was desperate, but Julia had every reason to hate her. Still, she whispered, "I need your help. I have nowhere else to go."

Julia's delicate eyebrows rose. Lexi wished she had the ability to communicate so much without speaking. She could almost feel the anger radiating from the other woman. But Julia's furrowed brow and pinched lips did nothing to detract from her beauty. She was thin, blonde and several inches taller than Lexi. The epitome of the Southern prom queen grown up. Lexi knew there was more to her than that. After all, she'd spent months researching every detail of Julia Callahan's life.

"You tried to take my son away from me." Julia shook her head. "Why would I have any inclination to help you?"

"I made sure you kept him in the end," Lexi said, adjusting her round glasses. "Don't forget I was the one who gave you the information that made the Johnsons rescind their custody suit."

"I haven't forgotten," Julia answered. "It doesn't explain why you're on the doorstep of my salon. Or what kind of help you need."

Lexi crossed her arms over her chest as her stomach began to roll. She should have stopped for breakfast on the way into town. "They found out it was me," she continued. "Dennis and Maria Johnson fired my father's firm as their corporate attorneys. Several of their friends followed. We lost over half our business."

Her voice faltered as memories of her father's rage and disappointment assaulted her. She cleared her throat. "In response, my dad made a big show of humiliating me in front of the entire firm. Then he officially fired and practically disowned me."

Lexi had worked for her father's firm since she graduated from law school six years ago. Following in his footsteps, doing whatever he expected, had been her overriding goal in life. She still lived in the apartment he'd paid for since college. Her eviction notice had come two days ago.

She drew a steadying breath. "He said he regretted the day I'd come into his life. That I'm nothing more than…"

"Your father is an ass." Julia's clear assessment almost made Lexi smile.

"True," she agreed, blinking against the sudden moisture in her eyes. "But he's all I have. Or had."

"What about other family?"

"I was adopted when I was six. I was in the foster-care system and barely remember my biological mother. My dad never married. He was an only child and my grandparents died years ago."

"Friends?"

"I have work acquaintances, country-club cliques and clients. I'm not very good at making friends."

"It's probably hard to be a backstabbing, underhanded, slimy lawyer and a good friend at the same time."

Although the words hurt, Lexi couldn't help but hear the truth in them. "I guess."

"Sheesh. That was a joke." Julia stepped past her and turned a key in the front door. "Lighten up, Lex."

Lexi followed her into the empty salon, the emotional roller coaster of the past week finally sending her off the rails. "Are you kidding?" she yelled. "I just told you that my life is destroyed because I saved you and your son. I have nothing. No job. No home. No friends. No family. And you want me to lighten up?"

Julia flipped on a bank of lights and turned. "Actually, I want you to tell me how I'm supposed to help. Other than playing the tiniest violin in the world in your honor. I appreciate what you did for me. But we both know you put me through hell trying to give custody of Charlie to my ex-boyfriend's family. That doesn't exactly make us long-lost besties."

"I want a fresh start."

"So make one."

"It's not that easy. As ridiculous as it sounds, I'm twenty-seven years old and my father has controlled every aspect of my life. Hell, he even handpicked a personal shopper to make sure I always projected the right image. The image he chose for me. Since the moment I came to live with him, I've wanted to make him happy, make him believe I was worthy of his love and the money he spent on me."

She ran her hands through her hair and began to pace between the rows of styling chairs. "I'd never done anything without his approval until I gave you that file. I don't regret it. You're a great mother and I feel awful about my part in the custody suit."

"You should," Julia agreed.

Lexi sighed. "If I could take it all back, I would. I know it was wrong. But helping you cost my father a lot. I thought he'd understand and forgive me."

"He still might."

"I don't know if I want him to. At least not on his terms. I don't want to be the same kind of attorney my dad is. I don't even know if I still want to be a lawyer. I need time to breathe. To figure out my next move. To make a choice in life for me, not because it's what's expected." She paused and took a breath. "I thought maybe you could understand that."

Julia studied her for a few moments. "Maybe I can."

Lexi swallowed her embarrassment and continued, "If I stay in Brevia for a few weeks, I could figure out my options. I don't want my father to find me. I don't think he's going to forgive me, but I do expect him to come looking. He likes the control and he's not going to give that up so easily."

She patted her purse. "I have five hundred dollars in cash. I don't want to use credit cards or anything to help him track me. Not yet."

"You're kind of freaking me out. Is he dangerous?"

Lexi ran her hand along the edge of a shelf of styling products. "Not physically. But I'm not strong enough yet to stand on my own. Who knows if I'll ever be. But I want to try. I liked Brevia when I was here. I admire you, Julia. Your fierceness and determination. I know you have no reason to help me, but I'm asking you to, anyway."

"And you couldn't have called on your way?"

"I'm sorry," Lexi said quickly. "I wasn't thinking. I just got in my car and started driving. This was the only place I could think of to go. But if you—"

Julia held up a hand. "This is probably more of my typical bad judgment, but I'll help you."

Lexi felt her knees go weak with relief. Julia Callahan was her first, last and only hope. She knew her father well enough to know he was punishing her. That when he felt as if she'd been gone long enough to learn her lesson, he'd pull her back. In the past, Lexi would have been scrambling to find a way to return to his good graces. Something had changed in her when she'd chosen her act of rebellion. From the start, she'd known he'd find out, and she'd understood there would be hell to pay. She also believed it couldn't be worse than the hell she called a life.

"Thank you," she whispered with a shaky breath. "I promise I won't be an imposition on your life. I could answer phones or sweep up hair—whatever you need."

"A job?" Julia looked confused. "I thought you needed moral support. You're an attorney, for Pete's sake. Why do you want to sweep the floors of a hair salon?"

"I'm licensed in North Carolina to practice, but if I register with the state's bar association, my father will find me. I told you, I need time."

"I'm going to make coffee. I need the caffeine." The stylist looked over her shoulder at Lexi. "Have you had breakfast? We keep a stash of granola bars in the break room."

Lexi followed her to the back of the building. "A granola bar would be great. And I really will help out with anything you need."

Julia poured grounds into the coffee filter and filled the machine with water. She turned back to Lexi, shaking her head. "We start renovations next week on the salon's expansion. I can't hire anyone right now."

"I get it. I appreciate the moral support. I guess."

"No wonder your father can manipulate you so easily. Your emotions are written all over your face. You need to work on a tough exterior if you want to do okay on your own. Fake it till you make it, right? I thought lawyers were supposed to be excellent bluffers."

Lexi slid into one of the folding chairs at the small table. "I'm not much of a bluffer. That's why I was usually behind the scenes. I'm good at details and digging up dirt."

"Yes, I remember," Julia answered drily.

"Do you know anyone who's hiring in Brevia? Just temporarily."

A slow smile spread across Julia's porcelain features. "Now that you mention it, I do know about an available job. One of the waitresses at the local bar had twins last night. They came about a month early and were practically born in the back of Sam's police cruiser."

"Are you thinking I'd make a good nanny?"

"I wouldn't wish that job even on you. I'm thinking you'd make a perfect cocktail waitress."

"I don't drink," Lexi said quickly.

"You have to serve the drinks. Not guzzle them yourself."

Lexi unwrapped the granola bar Julia handed to her, her empty stomach grumbling in anticipation. "I don't like those types of places."

"I don't like exercise," the other woman countered, "but I still run five days a week."

Lexi closed her eyes for a moment. Julia's quick wit and no-nonsense attitude were what she'd initially found so fascinating. Almost a year ago, Lexi and her father had been hired by their longtime clients Dennis and Maria Johnson to investigate Julia's life so they could try to take custody of her young son away from her. The boy's biological father was the Johnsons' son, Jeff.

Lexi knew if you threw enough money at a problem, it likely went away. But Julia had kept fighting. Sure, she had her problems, but Lexi had never seen someone stand up to people with so much power. Julia might have been faking her confidence some of the time, but it had made Lexi realize she didn't have to be her father's puppet forever.

Even if she owed him everything, didn't she still deserve to make choices in her own life? To live life on her terms? She had to at least try.

"Could the work last six weeks?"

"I think so. Amy is going to have her hands full, but I know she doesn't want to lose her job. She works at night, so she'll be able to manage around the babies once she gets back on her feet."

"It sounds good, although I don't have any experience as a waitress."

"Are you a quick learner?"

Lexi swallowed. "I made it through law school at the head of my class. I'm not sure how that applies to waitressing, but it's all I've got."

Julia watched her for another moment. "Are you sure you want to do this? It would be easier to go groveling to Daddy and beg him to give you back your cushy little life."

Lexi stood. "I want a real life."

"I know how that feels. I've got a place you can stay while you're in town. Let me text my receptionist to come in early, then we can get you settled." Julia took out her phone and began punching the keypad. "No offense, but you could use a shower and change of clothes."

Lexi looked down at her wrinkled pants and the stain of coffee on her collared button-down. "I stayed at a cheap motel off the interstate last night," she admitted. "The bathroom creeped me out too much to use this morning."

"Clearly." Julia finished her text, then grabbed a set of keys from a hook behind the door. "Are you ready?"

"As much as I appreciate your help, I can't possibly impose and stay at your house," Lexi argued.

"No doubt. You can have my apartment. With everything happening so quickly, I'm still on the lease. I've been subletting it to Sam's dad, but Joe and my mom got married a few weeks ago. The place is empty."

"Two family weddings in one year. Congrats, by the way."

Julia smiled. "Thanks. It's been a whirlwind but I'm happy."

"Your relationship with Sam really started as a fake arrangement to help with the custody case?"

"It did, but then it became so much more."

Lexi thought for a moment, then said, "I guess you could say that I'm partially responsible. Without the custody fight, who knows if or when you two would have gotten around to figuring out you're perfect for each other."

Julia laughed out loud. "Don't push your luck. I said I'd help you. I'll make sure you get the job, and sublet my apartment to you. I've got another three months on the lease. But as far as figuring out your life and growing a spine when it comes to your father, that's all you."

Lexi wondered if she'd ever be able to loosen her father's hold. In the past she hadn't realized how bad she wanted that. Now she did, and if this was her only chance to make it happen, she wasn't going to blow it.

She nodded, her throat tight with emotion. "I'm going to give it my best shot."

Scott Callahan heard the crash as he took another deep swallow from his glass of whiskey. He glanced toward the back of the bar as he jiggled the glass, determined to loosen every bit of liquor that clung to the melting ice.

"Sounds like she broke another one," he said to the waitress who brought him a third round. His instructions upon his first order were clear: as soon as his glass was empty, he was ready for another. No questions asked and there'd be a hefty tip at the end of the night. When Scott drank, he did it fast and he did it alone.

In his case, misery did not love company.

"New girl," the waitress answered. "The absolute worst I've ever seen." She put the fresh glass on the table and picked up his empty. "Julia vouched for her, but it's like she's never even held a tray. Luke is desperate for the help. Hell, he's desperate for a lot of things. But I don't know if we have enough glasses in the back to keep her around much longer."

Scott leaned back in his chair. "You said Julia vouched for her." He nodded toward the red-faced pixie who came around the back of the bar. "That little mouse is friends with Julia—uh, Morgan?"

"Julia Callahan now," the waitress corrected. "She married the town's police chief a few months back."

Scott nodded. "I'm happy for her. Do they make a good match?"

"Perfect." The woman's voice turned wistful. "Sam Callahan was the biggest catch this side of the county line. I never really pegged him for a family man. But he dotes on Julia's boy. It's true love."

"Good for them," Scott mumbled, not wanting to reveal his connection to Sam. He wrapped his fingers around the cool glass once more.

"How do you know Julia?"

He schooled his features into an emotionless mask. "Her hair salon."

"I haven't seen you in here before. You new to town?"

"Just passing through," he said and took a sip. "Thanks for the fresh drink."

"Sure." Realizing the conversation was over, the waitress walked away.

Scott had been in enough bars in his time to know that a good waitress could sense when a customer wanted to chat and when to leave him alone. He was glad he'd sat in the section he had. The little mouse waitress, cute as she was, didn't seem like someone who'd take a hint if you hung it around her neck. Not his type for certain.

He didn't know what he expected from Brevia, North Carolina. He looked around the bar's interior, from the neon signs glowing on the walls to the slightly sticky sheen on the wood floor. The bar ran along the back of the far wall although few stools were occupied. Not the most popular place in town, so no wonder there was a for-sale sign in the window. Still, the lack of customers suited him just fine. The watering holes he usually frequented in D.C. may have been classier and more historic. But as far as Scott was concerned, liquor was liquor and it didn't really matter who poured it or where.

He closed his eyes for a moment and wondered what had brought him to Brevia tonight. After the blowout he'd had with his brother, Sam, at their dad's wedding a few weeks ago, he'd vowed never to step foot in this town again. If he admitted the truth, he had no place else to go. No friends, no one who cared whether he showed up or not. His dad and brother might be the exception to that, but they were both too mad at him for it to matter now.

He drained his glass again. He liked the way alcohol

eventually numbed him enough so the dark thoughts hovering in the corners of his mind disappeared. Maybe it had led to some stupid decisions, but it also took the edge off a little. And Scott had a lot of edges that needed attention.

As a few more patrons wandered out, Scott's waitress came over to the table. "It's a slow night, honey," she told him. "I'm heading home. I could give you a ride somewhere or you could stop by my place for a nightcap."

She said it so matter-of-factly, Scott almost missed the invitation in her voice. He glanced up. "What's your name?"

"Tina."

He flashed the barest hint of a smile. "Tina, trust me. You can do way better than me on any given night. Even in a town like Brevia."

"I'm willing to take my chances." She surveyed him up and down. "I could wait years for a man who looks like you to walk into this place."

He took her hand in his and ran his finger across the center of her palm. "You deserve more than the likes of me. Go home, Tina." He pressed a soft kiss on her knuckles. "And thank you for the offer. It's a hard one to pass up."

She sighed. "Enjoy your night then."

He watched her walk away, then shifted his gaze as he felt someone watching him. The pixie of a waitress stood next to a table, her mouth literally hanging open as she gaped at him as if he was the big, bad wolf. A rush of heat curled up his spine. Maybe he should have taken Tina up on her offer. He was clearly in need of releasing some kind of pent-up energy.

He straightened from the table where he sat and lifted

his glass in mock salute, adding a slow wink for good measure.

The mouse snapped her rosebud lips together and spun around, sending another glass flying from the tray she balanced precariously in one hand.

Scott shook his head as the crash reverberated through the bar. That was her fifth for the night. A clumsy new waitress wouldn't last long.

He moved to a seat at the bar and ordered another round.

To his surprise, the bartender shook his head. "You've had enough, buddy."

"Excuse me?"

"I said I'm cutting you off."

Scott knew for a fact—almost a fact—that he never appeared drunk even when he was. It had been his downfall too many times to count. People assumed the idiot things he did weren't in direct relation to the amount of alcohol he'd consumed. "What the hell? I'm not making a scene. It's still early."

"It's 1:00 a.m."

"That means I've got an hour left."

"Not in my bar you don't. I own this place and I'm saying you're done here."

"What's the problem, man?"

The bar's owner was in his late forties, a tall, balding man with a lean face. Scott wasn't acting out of the ordinary, so couldn't figure out what was the problem.

"The problem," the bartender said as he leaned closer, "is that I saw you kissing my girlfriend's hand a few minutes ago. Now get the hell out of my bar."

Scott thought about the lovely Tina and cringed. "I

had no idea she was your girlfriend. She invited me over for a drink and—"

He didn't get to finish his sentence as the bartender grabbed at the scruff of his collar. Without thinking, Scott slammed the man's hand to the wooden counter, stopping just short of breaking it.

The bartender yelped in pain, then yanked his hand away.

"I told you," Scott repeated quietly, "I didn't know."

"Luke, is everything okay here?"

Scott turned and saw the tiny waitress standing at his side. She was even smaller up close, her big eyes blinking at him from behind round glasses. As far as he could tell, she didn't wear a speck of makeup, her pale skin clear without it other than a dusting of freckles across her nose and cheeks. Her red hair was pulled back into a severe ponytail at the nape of her neck. She bounced on her toes, looking warily from Scott to Luke.

"Everything's fine, Lexi," the bartender said coolly. "This customer has had enough. He's leaving."

"So Lexi's the bouncer?" Scott smiled at the mouse. "Are you going to throw me out?"

"You don't seem drunk," Lexi observed.

He knew the bartender was right even if he'd never own up to it. Scott wasn't much of a gambler, but he'd perfected a poker face. Nothing good ever came from admitting he'd had too much to drink. Especially at a bar. "I'm not," he answered, even though he knew it was a lie. "But I'd like to be." He settled into his chair and gave her a broad smile.

A streak of pink crept up from the neckline of her Riley's Bar T-shirt, coloring her neck and cheeks. A muscle in Scott's abdomen tightened. He imagined her entire petite frame covered in those sweet freckles and flushed pink with desire. For him.

Whoa. Where had that come from? He blinked several times to clear his head.

"Do you have something in your eye?" the mouse asked. "I have eyedrops in my purse if you need them."

So much for his charm with women. He was rusty these days. "No," he answered.

"He don't need anything," Luke interrupted. "He's on his way out."

"No wonder your bar is so run-down." Scott bit out a laugh. "If this is how you treat your customers…"

He saw Luke's eyes narrow a fraction. "My customers don't bad-mouth my bar. This establishment happens to be a local favorite."

Scott made a show of looking around at the nearly empty stools and tables. "I can see how popular you are. Yes, indeed." He glanced at the waitress, who gave a small shake of her head before dropping her gaze to the ground.

Somehow the disappointment he read in her eyes ground its way under his skin, making his irritation at being kicked out swell to full-fledged anger. He didn't know why it mattered, but suddenly Scott was determined not to let the bartender win this argument. Nobody in this one-horse town was going to get the best of him.

"I'm not leaving until I get another drink." He crossed his arms over his chest and dared the other man to deny him.

"Maybe you should just give him one more," Lexi suggested softly.

"No way." Luke reached for the phone hanging next

to the liquor bottles. "This loser is finished, one way or another." He pointed the receiver in Scott's direction. "I'll give the police a call. Tell them I've got a live one making a disturbance down here, and let them haul you away."

The last thing Scott needed was his brother finding him in a town bar tonight unannounced, let alone making trouble. Scott wanted to talk to Sam, but on his terms and in his own time frame.

Sam had moved to North Carolina several years ago and was definitely protective of his new hometown. Scott told himself he'd stopped caring about his brother's opinion years ago, but that didn't mean he wanted to go toe-to-toe with him tonight. He knew it would be easier to cut his losses and walk out now, but he couldn't do it. Not with Lexi and Luke staring at him. Backing down wasn't Scott's style, even when it was in his best interest.

His gaze flicked to the front door, then back to the bartender. "I noticed a for-sale sign in the window," he said casually.

Luke's eyes narrowed. "You in the market for a bar?"

"Someone could do a lot with this space. Make it more than some two-bit townie hangout."

"Is that so?" Luke crossed his arms over his chest. "Why don't you make me an offer, city boy?"

"Why don't you get me a drink and maybe I will."

A slow smile curved the corner of the bar owner's lips. He turned and grabbed a bottle off the shelf.

Lexi tugged on Scott's sleeve. "It's none of my business, but I don't think it's a good idea for you to discuss a possible business transaction now. You might want to wait until the morning."

"I think this is the perfect time," Scott said and leaned

closer to her, picking up the faint scent of vanilla. How appropriate for a woman who looked so innocent. "And you're right, it's none of your business."

The bartender placed a drink in front of Scott and clinked his own glass against it.

"Be that as it may," Lexi said, tugging again, "in order for a deal to hold up, there is the matter of due consideration. That won't apply if one or the other party is proved to be under the influence of drugs or alcohol."

Scott shrugged out of her grasp. "Honey, are you a waitress or a lawyer? Because you handle those big words a lot better than you do a tray of glasses."

"That's right." Luke's eyes lit up. "Julia said you were an attorney when she got me to hire you. Said you worked your way through law school waiting tables."

"She did?" Lexi had worked her way through law school clerking at her father's firm. She hadn't waited on anything other than an airplane before tonight. Still, she nodded. "I did. I am. An attorney, that is. I'm currently taking a break."

Scott eyed her. "As a cocktail waitress?"

Her lips thinned, which was a shame because he'd noticed they were full and bow-shaped. "For now."

Scott couldn't resist leaning closer again. "You might be the walking definition of the term 'don't quit your day job.'"

"You're a jerk," she whispered.

"Yes, I am."

Luke clapped his hands together. "This is perfect." He took a step back and flipped on and off the light switch next to the bar. "We're closing early, y'all," he shouted to the lone couple in a booth toward the back. "Clear out now."

Ignoring the groans of protest, he pointed to Lexi. "You can write up an offer for the pretty boy. Better yet, there's an old typewriter on my desk in the back. Grab it and you can make the contract."

She shook her head. "I don't think——"

"I'm not asking you to think," Luke barked. "You've broken a half-dozen glasses tonight. If you want to keep this job, get the damn typewriter."

She threw a pointed glance at Scott. "Are you sure this is what you want?"

Looking into her bright eyes, the only thing he could think of was that he wanted to kiss her senseless. But he sure as hell had a longer list of things he didn't want.

He didn't want the botched arrest at the U.S. Marshals Service that had taken his partner's life and put Scott on forced administrative leave. He didn't want the resignation letter burning a hole in his back pocket. He didn't want to go back to his empty condo in D.C. and stare at the yellow walls for days on end. He didn't want to feel so helpless and alone.

"Don't tell me you're all talk?" Luke slapped a wet towel onto the bar as he spoke. "I should have guessed you'd be willing to spout out big words but not follow up with any action. If you aren't serious, get the hell out of my bar. I've got better things to do than waste my time with this."

Scott spoke to the bar owner without taking his eyes from Lexi. "I'm all about action." He picked up his glass and drained it again. "Lexi, would you please get Luke's typewriter? We need to talk dollars for a few minutes. See how badly your good old boy really wants to sell."

Chapter Two

Scott felt someone poking at him, but couldn't force his eyes to open. "Go away," he mumbled.

A shower of ice-cold water hit his face. He sat up, sputtering and rubbing his hands across his eyes. Water dripped from his hair and chin.

"Rise and shine, Sleeping Beauty."

"I'm going to kill you," he said with a hiss of angry air, then looked around. He was on a worn leather couch in a small office, the shelves surrounding him dusty and lined with kitchen equipment. "Where am I?"

Sam handed him a towel. "You passed out. Luke Trujillo called me at three in the morning, laughing his butt off. He said he offered you a ride, but you insisted you wanted to spend the night in your bar. When did you get back into town?"

"Last night."

"You didn't call. Does Dad know you're here?"

"Not yet." Scott covered his eyes with the towel, under the guise of drying off his hair. "I didn't call because our last family get-together didn't exactly end on good terms."

Memories of the previous evening came back to him in full force. When he was certain he had his features schooled to a blank mask, he lowered the towel. "But I'm a big boy, Sam. You don't have to worry about me."

"Are you kidding?" His brother paced back and forth across the worn rug between the couch and an oversize oak desk on the far wall. "You didn't know where you were a minute ago."

"I was disoriented. It happens."

"What the hell were you thinking?"

"It was a misunderstanding. The guy was being a jerk about serving me, so I gave him a song and dance about wanting to buy this place."

Sam grabbed a piece of paper from the desk and shoved it toward Scott. "This isn't a song and dance. It's a contract for purchase and sale. You gave him a down-payment check for fifty grand. Luke has wanted to sell for over a year now. To hear him tell it, the place is a money pit. He's got family in Florida. Hell, he's probably already packing his bags."

As Scott read the words on the paper, his head pounded even harder. The contract had his signature on the bottom, along with Luke Trujillo's and one other. In neat, compact writing was the name Lexi Preston scrawled above the word *Witness* on the last line.

The pixie waitress-attorney from last night. Clear green eyes and the shimmer of red hair stole across his mind. Wanting to impress her. Wanting to keep drinking. His two main objectives from late last night. Now, in the harsh light of morning, he realized how stupid and impulsive he'd been.

Again.

Most of the trouble—and there was a lot of it—Scott had in life was a result of being impulsive. He led with his emotions, anger being the top of that list. Normally, he wouldn't let himself slow down enough to care about the consequences. But the botched arrest two months ago, a direct result of his poor judgment, had put him on the sidelines of his own life. It drove him crazy, although he wouldn't have that discussion with Sam.

"I know you're still getting a paycheck and Dad says you've done well on investments, but it's a lot of cash, Scott. What are you going to do when you go back to the Marshal Service? I don't want to see you throw your money away like this."

Sam was the by-the-book brother, the one who'd always done the right thing. The responsible Callahan. At least, that was how it had been after their mother died. But a lot of years had passed since then. Scott was a grown-up now and he wasn't about to admit that he'd messed up yet again.

"I bought a bar. So what?" He threw the towel onto the floor by the couch and combed his hands through his hair. "I can afford it."

"That's not the point," his brother argued.

"Sam, I'm a big boy. I know what I'm doing. Maybe it doesn't make sense to you, but you're going to have to trust me on this." He walked past his brother and down the short hall to the bar's main room. He couldn't let Sam see how in over his head he felt. He'd done a lot of stupid things in his life, but last night might take the cake. What had felt warm and inviting then now just looked in need of a good scrubbing. The wood floors were scratched and dull and the tables mismatched, several sporting a layer of grime years thick. The place definitely had more charm in the half dark.

"I don't have much of a reason to trust you, and I definitely don't trust Lexi Preston."

Scott spun around, then winced as the abrupt movement made his head hurt more. "What about Lexi?" he asked, not willing to address the issue of trust between him and Sam this early in the morning.

"She represented the family who tried to take away Charlie from Julia."

"I don't understand." Scott had immediately fallen for Julia's toddler son. He didn't know Julia well, but it was clear she was a natural mother. "I thought the ex-boyfriend's family was from Ohio. What's the attorney doing in Brevia? Julia got full custody."

Julia had been embroiled in the custody case when she and Sam were first together. Being with Julia had stopped Sam from taking a job Scott had helped arrange for him with the U.S. Marshals. It had been Scott's big attempt to repair his relationship with his brother, and it had felt like one more rejection when Sam had chosen Julia instead. Scott hadn't quite forgiven her for that, but it hadn't prevented him from forming a quick affection for the boy.

Sam shook his head, frustration evident in the tense line of his shoulders. "I don't understand, either. She got to town yesterday with some sob story about how she needs a fresh start. Julia may talk tough but she's a total softy at heart. She helped Lexi get the job and is renting the woman her old apartment."

"Keep your friends close and your enemies closer?" Scott asked, his mind suddenly on sharp alert. Julia was family now. He protected family, even if his methods were sometimes unorthodox.

Sam shook his head. "I want that woman to stay away from all of us. I don't like the fact that she was involved in this mess with you."

Scott bristled at Sam's condescending tone. "I told you, I can take care of myself. I don't know if she has ulterior motives coming to town, but Lexi Preston didn't influence my decision to buy this bar."

"She let you enter into a contract when you were drunk."

"Who said I was drunk last night? Maybe I bought this place as an investment. It's an historic building and—"

"You're not fooling me. I know the Marshals incident messed with your head. I know you've been drinking more than normal and your normal is pretty damn much." Sam took a step closer. "I think you need help."

Blood roared through Scott's head. He hadn't been back in Brevia twenty-four hours and Sam was already starting another referendum on how messed up he was. He couldn't afford to debate whether it was true. Not yet.

"Get out." He spoke the words slowly, without any of the emotion swirling through his gut.

"Scott, listen—"

"No, Sam, you listen." Scott began straightening chairs around the various tables, needing something—anything—to do with his hands. Needing to take some action. "The incident didn't mess with my head. It killed a good man. Maybe I use alcohol to dull the memories of that more than I should. But I'm not out of control.

I walked away when it was clear that part of the internal investigation meant me smearing my dead partner's reputation. I don't know right now if I'll go back. So I bought this place. It's an investment. Not one that you would make, but it's my money and my life. Back off. Go home to Julia and Charlie. I don't need you here."

The sound of the chairs scraping against the wood floor gave welcome relief to the silence that stretched between the brothers. Finally, Scott stopped and looked over. "I mean it. I'm fine."

Sam gave a curt nod. "I'm here, Scott. When you do need me, I'm here." He turned and walked out of the bar into the bright morning.

As the door swung shut behind him, Scott turned a chair around and sank into it, massaging his forehead with two fingers.

What the hell was he going to do now?

Lexi tried to ignore the pounding on the apartment door. As she stared, arms folded tightly across her chest, the noise grew. Had her father had a change of heart already, prepared to forgive her supposed lapse in judgment if she came home and continued to do his bidding? It was late morning and she'd already unpacked her few belongings and made a run to the local grocery for essential supplies. As silly as it seemed, she'd just gotten a taste of freedom and didn't want to give it up so soon.

She also didn't want her neighbors to worry or, worse, call Julia or Sam. Taking a fortifying gulp of air, she turned the knob and opened the door.

Oh.

Oh, dear.

Scott Callahan loomed in the doorway, irritation and

a healthy five-o'clock shadow etched on his handsome face. He was still wearing the same casual sweater and wrinkled jeans from the night before. She looked for the resemblance to Julia's husband, Sam, figuring it was too much of a coincidence to have two Callahans in the same small town.

She'd been shocked when he'd told her his name as she was putting together the contract for sale last night. Although Scott's hair was dark, the two men shared the same brilliant blue eyes, strong jaw and towering height that made them both intimidating and undeniably male.

She took an involuntary step back, hating the blush creeping up her cheeks. Why did this man rattle her so much?

That was easy enough to answer. Just the sight of him made her long-dormant imagination kick into high gear. His hair just grazed his collar, his blue eyes made brighter by the contrast to long lashes that any woman would envy. He was beautiful, the kind of handsome that would attract female attention wherever he went.

Men who looked like Scott Callahan didn't notice Lexi, and last night he'd certainly noticed her. At least it had felt that way. He'd leaned in and his eyes had caught on her mouth as if he wanted to kiss her. She'd imagined what that kiss would feel like as she lay in her bed in the wee morning hours, watching dawn through the curtains in her bedroom. She could almost taste his lips on hers even now.

Now.

She blinked and cleared her throat. "What are you doing here?"

He lifted one long arm to rest on the door frame, muscles bunching under his sweater. A smile played at the corner of his mouth. He seemed a lot less irritated than he had a few moments earlier. "What's your story, Lexi Preston? You look shy and talk like an academic, but you've got a wild side. I can tell."

She hugged her arms more tightly around herself. "You can tell no such thing."

"I can tell you want me to kiss you."

She sputtered, "I do not."

"Liar." He took a lazy step toward her. "But that's not going to happen. Yet."

Lexi was shocked by the ripple of disappointment that rolled through her. "What do you want?" she repeated. "I'm guessing this isn't an official employee meeting."

He pulled a sheet of paper out of his back pocket. "I want to know why you let me sign this damn contract."

"You told me to write it up. I didn't let you do anything. In fact, I advised you not to sign it."

"I was drunk."

She cocked her head to one side and studied him. The rumpled clothes, the hint of bruising under his eyes. "You said you weren't."

"I hide it well."

No wonder he'd been flirting with her. It was the alcohol, not attraction. Of course. A guy as hot as Scott would definitely need beer goggles to flirt with her. "I warned you about due consideration. You assured me you were in full control of your faculties and able to make a rational decision."

"I want out." He came all the way into the apartment, filling it with his large, muscular body and...sheesh, she had a one-track mind.

"The bank has to draw up the final contract. Maybe you won't be approved for the loan."

"I can guarantee I'll be approved, so I want out now."

A whistle sounded from behind her. "It's not that easy." She turned on her heel and padded to the kitchen, pulling two cups from the cabinet. She dropped a tea bag in each and poured the hot water. Turning back, she handed one to Scott. He eyed it suspiciously. "What's this?"

"Green tea. It helps me think." She took a small sip. "Explain to Luke Trujillo that you were inebriated last night. The contract won't hold up if you signed it under the influence. I'm sure Tina will vouch for how many drinks you had over a normal limit."

"That's the problem. No one can know I was drunk."

"Why not?"

He brought the mug to his mouth, sniffed and made a face. "You're kidding with this, right? Where's the coffee?"

"I don't drink coffee. Green tea is full of antioxidants."

"You're an attorney and a health nut? That's some combination."

"My father says... Never mind." She took another drink. "Don't be a baby. It's just tea." She studied him intently. "Why do you want to hide that you were drunk?"

"I'm not a baby," he said and took a huge gulp of tea. "That's disgusting."

"You're avoiding my question."

"You're such a lawyer." He shook his head and reached around her to place the mug on the counter. "My brother's already given me grief about last night. I don't need him on my back for anything else."

"Are the two of you close?"

"Not a bit."

She raised the cup to her lips again, then lowered it as her mind raced. "If you're not close, why do you—"

"It's complicated."

Lexi could just imagine. She'd known him for less than twenty-four hours, but Scott Callahan was already the most intriguing man she'd ever met. At first glance he was all alpha-male bravado, but she sensed something more. His eyes had a haunted look that wasn't related to a hangover, but might have everything to do with a bone-deep loneliness. The kind of lonely people felt if they thought no one in the world truly loved them. As if they had no home.

The kind of lonely Lexi often saw reflected in her own eyes.

She had nothing in common with this man, but she wanted to reach out to him. She yearned to understand what made someone who appeared so sure of himself at the same time give off waves of uncertainty.

She wanted to really know him.

As if he could read her intention, his eyes turned cold. "Never mind. I'll figure something out." His voice cut through her thoughts. "Luke gave me a fair price and I've got the time and money to deal with it. Maybe I'll redo the whole thing and sell it for a hefty profit." His words were sure but his tone still held a hint of uncertainty.

"If you didn't want to own a bar, why did you buy it?"

"I don't know." He ran his hand through his almost-black hair. "I'm known for being impulsive. It's my trademark."

There must be more to the story, but as much as she wanted to know, it wasn't any of her business. Yet. "I never do anything impulsive."

"That's not how I heard it." He glanced over her

shoulder at the tray of half-full glasses sitting on the kitchen table. "Here you are, a fancy-pants corporate attorney, renting my sister-in-law's apartment, practicing to be a bar waitress in this sleepy Southern town. Are you telling me this is some sort of master plan?"

She almost smiled. "I guess you're right. I've been pretty impulsive in the last couple of days."

He shook his head. "That wasn't a compliment."

"I'm going to take it as one, anyway." She placed her mug on the counter. When she turned back, Scott had stepped closer. Too close. Close enough that she could smell toothpaste on his breath and the musky scent of last night's cologne on his shirt.

"If you want to get impulsive, I can help." He reached his hand up and trailed the pad of his thumb along her jaw. "I'm an expert at impulsive."

"I'm not that kind of girl," she whispered, hating that he broke straight through to her earlier longing.

"I can't figure out what kind of girl you are." His mouth turned up at the corner. "But I know you're the worst waitress I've ever seen." He straightened, dropping his hand. "I'm the boss now. So you'd better practice all day with those glasses. Because you helped get me into this mess and I'm not going to let you cost me more money every night. Luke may have owed Julia a favor, but I don't owe anyone anything."

Lexi sucked in a breath. "Are you threatening to fire me?"

"It's no threat," Scott told her. "I'm sure you've got a corner office waiting for you somewhere. I don't care why you're slumming it in a bar. But it's mine now. I don't play favorites. Show up a half hour early for your shift tonight. We're having an employee meeting."

He turned and headed for her door.

"This is because you're mad that I wrote the contract. You want to blame me. It's not fair."

He held up one hand and ticked off several points. "I'm mad that I signed the contract. I blame myself for that, but I don't appreciate you being a part of that moment. And if you haven't realized it before, life isn't ever fair. Deal with it."

Without looking back, he strode from her apartment, slamming the door shut behind him.

Chapter Three

By five o'clock that night, Scott's headache was way beyond a hangover. He'd driven down to Charlotte to pick up some updated electronics the bar needed right away, along with a few extra clothes until he had time to get to his condo in D.C. for his stuff. He'd noticed a bathroom and shower off the office in back, where he'd bunk until he could figure out what to do with his new investment.

Damn. His plan hadn't included staying in Brevia for more than a few days, and definitely not in this run-down bar. He didn't know why he'd come in the first place, other than wandering around D.C. and watching ESPN in his place had been driving him crazy.

He and Sam hadn't been close in years, and he knew his brother still didn't trust him after Scott's part in breaking up Sam's first engagement. He pressed two fingers to the side of his head as the pain of regret mingled with the dull pounding inside his brain.

He'd thought they were going to put the past behind them when Sam was planning to take the job with the Marshals, but the relationship with Julia had ended that. Scott had been mad as hell. He'd stuck his neck out to get Sam the job. Although he didn't want to admit it, he'd craved a second chance at a relationship with his brother.

He knew Sam didn't want him here. Maybe that had been part of the motivation for making this stupid deal. He'd always had a talent for getting under his brother's skin.

Hefting another box of beer bottles into the large refrigerator in the back room of the bar, he spun on his heel as someone cleared his throat behind him.

Scott slammed the refrigerator door and faced a craggy-looking man whose thin blond hair was pulled back into a ponytail at the nape of his neck. He looked to be in his mid-forties and wore faded jeans and an army-green canvas jacket over a white T-shirt.

"You ain't Luke," the man told him.

"Great observation." Scott eyed the stranger, clearly ex-military by the way he held himself. "I'm Scott Callahan, the new owner of this place."

"New owner?" The man's eyes narrowed. "I didn't hear nothing about a new owner."

"It's a recent development." He'd also met earlier with Luke, who'd been thrilled to hand over his keys. He'd offered to stick around for a few weeks to help, but Scott had declined. From what he'd seen this morning going through the bar's accounts and ledgers, Luke hadn't known much about running a business. Scott had certainly spent enough time in bars. He figured he could pick up most of what he needed to know from the staff. As long as he kept the beer cold and the liquor flowing, how hard could it be?

"You can't be any worse than Luke. That guy could barely tap a keg when he got here."

"I've tapped plenty of kegs in my day," Scott assured him. "I didn't catch your name."

The two of them stared at each other for several moments. Finally, the man said, "I'm Jon Riley."

"As in Riley's Bar?" Scott tried not to look surprised.

Joe nodded. "My dad opened this place almost twenty years ago. Luke took over when Dad passed a few years back."

"I'm sorry. You work here?"

"Unfortunately." When Scott didn't reply, Jon continued, "I've worked in restaurants most of my life. Trained as a chef up in New York. But I got hurt over in Iraq and, well…ended up back here."

Scott had noticed the full kitchen, although from the looks of it, nothing had been cooked there for years. "Riley's doesn't serve food."

"Used to when my dad had it." Jon shrugged. "Now I wash glasses, clean up, handyman stuff. Whatever needs doing. You gonna change things around?"

"I've owned the place for less than twenty-four hours. My head is still swimming." And pounding.

"That didn't answer the question."

"You've still got a job if you want one."

"I do." Jon stuck out his bony hand and Scott shook it. "Nice to meet you, boss."

"You, too, Jon."

"I got one more question for you." Jon nodded toward the unused kitchen space. "My apartment's only an efficiency. I can't cook anything worth eating. I clock in here at six-thirty most nights. Would you mind if I brought in some supplies and made myself dinner before I started? I'll keep it clean."

"Is that what you've been doing?"

"Nope." His gaze dropped to the ground. "Luke didn't want to deal with it or have customers smelling my meals, but—"

"I don't care what you do in the kitchen. I'm not using it. We're having a staff meeting in a few minutes. Be great if you could be there."

"Thanks." Jon shrugged out of his coat. "I'm going to get started moving last night's empties."

Scott nodded, feeling overwhelmed by the task in front of him. He liked the fact that he was moving, at least. It gave him less time to think about what he couldn't do. Like his real job.

He heard voices at the front of the building. He glanced out to see four women, including Lexi, come through the entrance. He'd contacted the five waitresses and two male bartenders from the employee records he'd found in the desk. One of the women had just had a baby, which explained Lexi's hire. Both of the guys had come in right after lunch to go over things. Scott had asked the waitresses to meet just before they opened tonight. He had no idea what he was going to say to them. Should he give a football-huddle pep talk or beg for help? He'd never been an employer. Never had to worry about anyone on the job but himself. That was about to change. He had his first employee meeting to run.

"Hello, ladies," he called with more confidence than he felt. "How is everyone doing tonight?"

All four women stopped and stared at him. He recognized Tina from last night, her gaze still an open invitation. Lexi looked wary, making eye contact with everything except him. The other two women he didn't recognize. He'd left messages for both of them earlier, so he didn't know what they thought of the change in ownership.

He stepped forward. "I'm Scott Callahan, the new owner of Riley's Bar."

"I'm Misty," the first woman told him. She was older for a bar waitress—early fifties if he had to guess. Her jet-black hair curled on top and was held back by a shiny clip. She couldn't have been more than five feet tall. It was hard to imagine her hefting a tray of glasses. But that remained to be seen.

"I appreciate all of you coming in."

Tina gave him a slow smile. "I didn't know you were going to buy the place."

Scott returned her smile. "I didn't know Luke was your boyfriend when you invited me for a drink."

She shrugged. "We're on a break."

"I'm single." The fourth waitress piped up. "My name's Erin." The young woman sidled up to him. "I've been here awhile, so I can help you with anything you need." She wrapped her long fingers around his wrist. "Anything."

He heard Lexi snort as he unhooked his wrist and stepped away from Erin. He felt like more of a fraud as he tried to think of what they'd want a new boss to say. "I'm going to do my best to make Riley's Bar the spot for nightlife. I think there are a lot of opportunities for improvement."

"You can say that again," Misty agreed.

"First and foremost, we need to take care of our customers—both current and potential. I'm going to be making some changes that will help with that."

"What kind of changes?"

"Making this place look a little better for one thing. Nightly specials, more events to get locals and visitors in the door. It's your job to keep them happy once they're here. I want good customer service. Be attentive but not overbearing."

"Do we let them hit on us?" All the women but Lexi giggled. She looked horrified.

"Only if you want them to." He smiled. "But I'd prefer you kept your time here professional."

The three experienced waitresses nodded, while Lexi continued to look straight ahead. She seemed as nervous as a deer at a shooting range.

"What about tips?" Tina asked. "Luke used to take part of what we got because he made the drinks."

"He skimmed your tips?" Scott didn't know why this surprised him. He'd checked the liquor on the shelves earlier and found several bottles watered down. Apparently, Luke hadn't been cutting corners only on the alcohol.

"He said it was his fair share," Misty offered.

"What's fair is that you keep the money you make." Scott stepped behind the counter. "Most nights I'm going to be handling the bar. Max and Jasper, the other bartenders, will fill in as needed."

"You know how to mix a decent Tom Collins?" Misty asked.

Scott nodded. "I can mix almost anything." He had spent time as a bartender when he'd been younger and had picked up a thing or two from his favorite haunts in D.C.

They watched him as if they expected more. He'd called them in here, but now had no pearls of wisdom to dispense. Basically, he'd wanted to see what he was working with. Other than Lexi, they all looked competent and at home in the bar.

He pulled shot glasses down from a shelf and grabbed a bottle of Jack Daniel's. He needed something to take the edge off. Just one. He turned to the man standing in the doorway. "We're going to have a round to welcome the new owner. Join us?"

Jon Riley shook his head. "No, boss. I'm five years sober."

Scott's hand paused in pouring. "Sorry. I didn't know."

"It's fine," Jon said quietly and disappeared through the door.

"I don't want one, either," Lexi told him when he pushed four of the small glasses forward.

"You on the wagon, too?" Tina asked.

"I don't think it's a good idea to drink while working."

Scott felt a hot burst of irritation skim along his spine. He didn't need to be judged by his little mouse of a waitress. "It's a special occasion," he told her. "Maybe if you relax, you won't have so much trouble keeping the glasses on the tray instead of the floor."

She narrowed her eyes. "I'll be fine. Thanks." With a huff, she followed Jon.

"Anyone else got a problem?"

In response, the remaining waitresses each picked up a shot glass. They toasted and downed the whiskey. It burned his throat, but after a moment the familiar warmth uncurled in his stomach.

"Thanks, boss," Misty told him and headed toward the back behind Lexi.

The other two women left the glasses on the bar and after a bit of small talk, meandered out the front door. Lexi and Misty were the two working tonight.

When he was alone again, Scott cleaned up the glasses and wiped down the top of the bar. He stared for a moment at the whiskey Lexi hadn't drunk. It seemed a shame to waste perfectly good alcohol, so he quickly downed it before putting the glass in the stack to be washed.

He turned to see Lexi watching him from the side of the bar. "Do you think that's a good idea?" she asked quietly.

"Sweetheart, none of this is a good idea." He returned the bottle of Jack to the shelf. "Luckily, I'm not much one for caring. If it feels right, I go for it."

"And drinking on the job feels right to you?" She took a step closer. "It seems to me that's what got you this bar in the first place." She pulled the apron in her hands over her head and reached behind her back to tie it, causing her breasts to push against the soft material of her light pink T-shirt.

Scott sucked in a breath. Hell, the T-shirt wasn't even formfitting and its conservative crew-neck collar practically covered half her throat. Misty was wearing a low-cut, skintight number that barely held in her ample chest. But it hadn't had any effect on him. Unlike Lexi's buttoned-up outfit.

He walked around the edge of the bar and took her arm, spinning her away from him.

"What are you doing?" she said with a gasp.

"Helping you," he answered and tied her apron strings

together. "It seems to me the reason I'm in this mess is because of you and your contract."

"You wanted to buy the bar," she argued.

"I wanted to pick a fight with Luke," he countered, resting his hands on her hips, unable to resist circling his thumbs against the place where her shirt hem met the fabric of her black dress slacks. Attorney clothes, clearly made of expensive material. Not the sort of pants someone wore to serve drinks.

Which reminded him that Lexi wasn't the sort of woman who should be waitressing in a bar. "If it wasn't for your ever-helpful legal skills, we would have exchanged some big talk and called it a night. Now I've got a business I don't want in a town I don't want to live in."

She went perfectly still, whether because of his words or his touch, Scott didn't know. But her voice was breathless when she spoke. "Maybe you should have stopped to think before you agreed to anything. Maybe if your ego wasn't so big you would have left when he told you to go."

Ouch. Scott didn't want to admit how close to home that hit. The phrase *if you'd stopped to think* could have saved him so many different times in his life.

"I never do," he said quietly. "Stop. Or think."

Because then he might remember how lonely he always felt, how afraid he was of needing someone and being left alone, the way both his parents had done when he was a kid.

"You should try it sometime," she said, her voice just a whisper.

"What's done is done." He pulled her closer to him and whispered against her ear, "It's easier to do what people expected of me—which isn't much."

* * *

Lexi felt her heart squeeze tight. It was so quiet in the bar at the moment. She was surrounded by Scott, the warmth of his chest against her back and his spicy, soapy scent mingling with the tangy smell of liquor on his breath.

That was what did it, brought her back to her right mind. The alcohol was the only explanation for why he seemed to want to touch her as much as she wanted to be touched by him.

She drove her elbow back, surprised at how quickly he moved to block the shot. "You're messing with me—"

She stopped when the front door opened and half a dozen men walked through. One called out, "There's an under-new-management sign in the window. What's that about?"

Another gave a long whistle. "Hey, there's a flat screen now. Is that new?"

"I'll be watching you tonight," Scott whispered to her. "Just remember that."

Her mouth went dry as he turned away.

"Put it up today, boys," he answered. "Got cable set up, too. Have a seat and we'll find a game to watch."

A round of cheers went up and the men came over to shake Scott's hand. They moved toward a table, but he pointed to the other side of the room. "You're going to have a better view over there, fellows."

He'd moved them from her section to Misty's, but only smiled as Lexi glared at him.

She spilled one glass the entire night, a huge improvement from her first shift. She didn't have the natural gift of gab that Misty did, flirting and making small talk with the customers. But Lexi did her best to keep up, making sure she got every order right and moving as quickly as her legs could carry her.

She was getting used to the noise and the smell of the bar, the customers who got more boisterous as the night wore on. Lexi didn't have a lot of experience with boisterous. Her father's idea of out of control was playing opera music instead of something mellower during dinner. Even in college, Lexi had stayed away from bars, worried there was something in her, some sort of predisposition for addiction, like her biological mother had had.

Her dad had told her in great detail about how she would have to overcome the deficiencies in her gene pool throughout her life. He'd made her believe that if she got too close to the wild life that had killed her mother, she might end up down that same dark path. She had only a few snippets of memory of her birth mom. The scent of her musky perfume and being left alone in their small apartment for long periods of time. But she was curious about "the other side of life," as her dad called it.

Being in Riley's Bar, serving customers, was a revelation to Lexi. She didn't really have a desire to drink, but the energy from the people around her made her feel more alive than she ever had.

Scott took a shot with another customer. She didn't know how much he'd had tonight and it wasn't any of her business. He didn't seem wasted, although he hadn't last night, either. She still knew he was trouble. He tempted her to be different than the person she'd worked so hard to become. The way he made her feel could be dangerous to her very soul. She wanted an adventure, but how far was she willing to go to get a real one?

The bar emptied soon after the football game was

over, which she figured was normal. She took off her apron and hung it in the back hall, counting the money from the front pocket. She'd made twenty dollars in tips. Not a lot, but the cash meant more to her than any paycheck she'd ever received from her father's firm.

"You did better tonight."

She turned to see Jon Riley in the doorway that led to the unused kitchen. "I practiced carrying drinks around all day," she said with a grin.

"It worked." He returned her smile. "You're not a natural but you'll get there."

"My mom was a waitress her whole life," Lexi said, then wondered why she'd shared that.

"There's worse ways to make a living."

She thought about her father and the underhanded legal deals he'd gotten into the habit of arranging to keep his firm on top. Maybe that was a type of addiction in its own right. She'd never made a connection between her adoptive father and her biological mother, and the thought made her skin crawl the tiniest bit.

"She was an alcoholic," Lexi blurted. "Lost custody of me when I was six. Working in bars killed her."

Jon shook his head. "The booze killed her. You're not like that."

"How do you know?" Lexi asked, suddenly needing reassurance from this virtual stranger.

"I've been down that road," he said simply. "I can recognize a person battling demons. Sometimes it's easier to drown yourself than work on what's really wrong."

She heard Misty's laughter ring out from the front of the bar, followed by the deep tone of Scott's voice.

Jon jerked his head toward the sound. "That boy has

a war waging inside him. He's got a good heart but he's going to have to do some digging to find it again."

"Can someone like him be helped?"

The man shrugged. "Maybe. But they've got to want it. And you've got to risk that if they don't, you're gonna be real hurt trying for 'em."

She thought again about her mother, wondered what her demons had been and if anyone had tried to help her.

The door to the front of the bar swung open and Misty's head popped through. "Scott poured an extra glass of wine. Want to join me for a drink?"

Lexi turned her head. "I think…" She paused and glanced back over her shoulder. Jon had disappeared into the kitchen again. "I'm going to head home now."

Misty shrugged. "Your call. Nice work tonight. Scott thinks you're too slow but I could see you busting your hump the whole time."

Lexi felt color rise to her cheeks. Scott thought she was too slow. She'd been worrying about how to help him, and he'd been talking trash about her. She swallowed against the embarrassment rising in her throat. "Have a good night, Misty," she said. Grabbing her purse from the hook, she headed for the back door.

She wrapped her arms around herself against the cool night air. Fall temperatures were dipping, even here in the South. She hurried to her car, and once back in her apartment, slipped off her shoes. Her feet ached, her shoulders were sore. Most of her body hurt from using muscles she'd never dealt with before. She wore heels as an attorney but never spent hours standing.

Even though it was late, she ran a bath and slipped into the warm water, letting it soak away some of her aches and pains. She liked to be clean. That was one thing she did remember from the time before Robert Preston had adopted her. She'd spent a lot of time dirty.

The bathtub in Julia's apartment might not be large or fancy like the deep soaker she'd left behind, but it did the trick. By the time she put on her soft cotton pajamas, she felt relaxed again.

She'd padded to the kitchen for a glass of water before bed when she heard the soft knock on the door. This time she didn't worry that it might be her father. From the way her stomach dipped, she knew who was waiting on the other side.

Chapter Four

"It's late, Scott." She hated that her voice sounded breathless. "What do you want?"

"I need a place to sleep."

His tone held none of its usual teasing or cocky certainty. But she kept the door open only a crack, not yet willing to let him in. "I thought you were staying at the bar."

"Too damn quiet after everyone leaves. Too empty. And it smells like a bar."

She smiled a little. "You smell like a bar."

"I could use a shower." He lifted a black duffel bag into view. "I brought a change of clothes."

She shook her head. "You should stay with Sam and Julia."

"They're a family. I don't belong there."

"You don't belong here."

He shrugged. "I don't belong anywhere." Lexi knew it was the first wholly honest thing he'd said since they'd met. The smallest bit of vulnerability flashed in his eyes and she was a goner.

Jon Riley's words about being hurt echoed in her head, but she pushed them away as she reached out and took Scott's hand. Pulling him to her, she brushed a wayward lock of hair away from his forehead. Her finger traced the side of his face, much the same way he'd done the last time he touched her. Did it have the same effect? His heated gaze gave her hope that it did.

He looked as if he wanted to devour her, but didn't make a move. He only watched as she explored his skin with her hands, his chest rising and falling with shallow breaths.

"Misty said you think I'm too slow," she told him softly, the words stinging her pride as she repeated them.

"The customers don't seem to mind," he answered. "You made good tips tonight."

"So you're not going to fire me?" She tried to make her voice sound teasing.

"Not yet," he answered.

"I'd threaten you with a sexual-harassment lawsuit but you flirt with everyone at the bar except me. Why is that?"

"You're the one pressed up against me." He shifted, somehow drawing her closer without pulling her to him. "Who's doing the harassing?"

He was right, but she could sense that his need matched her own. In the quiet intimacy of her apartment, it made her bold enough to ask, "Does this feel like harassment, Scott?"

"This feels like heaven," he whispered. "But I didn't come here for this. I'm no good for you."

"That's the point. I'm looking for a wild adventure and developing a new fondness for things that aren't good for me."

He took her arms and lifted them around his neck. Her head tilted and he brushed his lips against hers. Finally. It seemed as if she'd been waiting for this kiss her entire life.

And it was worth it.

His mouth felt delicious, the pressure sending sparks of desire along every inch of her skin. She lost herself in the sensations, reeling from the onslaught of need he aroused in her.

His strong arms wrapped around her, pulling her more tightly against him until she could tell how much he wanted her. She wanted him with the same need, like a drug she couldn't get enough of. She was quickly tipping out of control and the unfamiliarity of that made her push away.

Lexi Preston never lost control. She knew the dark and dangerous path where that might lead.

"You're right," she said around a gulp of air. "I'm slow." She covered her still-tingling lips with her fingers for a moment and stared at the floor. "I'm not one of your usual barflies."

"I never thought you were."

She pulled her shirt hem down where it had bunched around her waist. "You can stay here tonight." She still didn't meet his gaze. "On the couch. There's no furniture in the second bedroom right now. Use the shower, whatever you need. I'm going to bed." She squeezed her eyes shut tight. "Alone."

Before he could answer, she turned and retreated to the bedroom.

Scott watched her go, willing his heart to slow and his body to settle down.

What the hell was he doing in Lexi's apartment?

He'd told her the truth—he'd come here to sleep. After the last stragglers had gone home, he'd sat alone at the empty bar with a glass of Jack Daniel's in his hand, ready to blot out the memories that flooded him when he closed his eyes. But he couldn't lift the drink to his lips.

Sam was right—he'd been doing more self-medicating with alcohol than he should lately. Since his partner had been killed, it was the only thing that numbed the pain and the thoughts that raced around his brain. He'd always enjoyed a good buzz, but he'd never needed it the way he did now.

He'd already lost control in so many areas of his life. How much was he willing to give up? He'd poured out the glass of whiskey and paced the length of the building. There was nothing more depressing than an empty bar after closing, when the lack of body heat and voices made it feel like a sad, lonely shell of broken dreams.

A lot like his life.

He'd gotten in his truck and driven here. Sure, he could have called Tina or even Misty and found a warm welcome and a warmer bed. Instead he'd craved the lightness he felt radiating from Lexi. She was the purest person he'd met in a long time, someone good and innocent and everything he hadn't been in years.

He didn't understand his need for her. He'd never been

attracted to the buttoned-up type before. But her straw-berry hair, big luminous eyes and creamy skin made him want to fold her into him and not let go.

Except he knew he'd destroy the goodness in her. That was what he did to the people he needed. As much as he might want her, he'd keep his distance. He'd stay on the couch, stay away from her bed. As self-destructive as he could be, he still had a deep need to protect the people around him. Too bad he was the person Lexi needed protection against the most.

Scott slept better on the overstuffed couch than he had in years. He woke, showered and dressed, feeling halfway human again.

By the time eight o'clock rolled around, Lexi still hadn't made an appearance. He knocked softly on her bedroom door. "I know you're awake. I hear you moving around. You can come out—I won't bite."

He heard something bang behind the closed door.

"I bet you have to go to the bathroom pretty bad by now."

The door opened and Lexi appeared, fully dressed in jeans and a shapeless T-shirt that nonetheless gave him a little thrill. She tried hard to hide her petite figure and he couldn't understand why.

"Why are you still here?" she asked warily.

"It's cheery."

"There isn't a lick of decoration in the place," she said and nudged him out of the way, slamming the bathroom door behind her.

He chuckled and moved back toward the kitchen, call-ing over his shoulder, "It's a hell of a lot cheerier than the bar."

He opened several cabinet doors. "There's got to be coffee here somewhere," he said as she came into the kitchen behind him.

"I told you I don't drink coffee. Tea is your only choice."

He made a choking sound.

"There's a bakery around the corner." She rolled her eyes. "Have at it."

"I have a better idea," he told her. "Let's grab breakfast. That diner in town is always crowded."

Her eyebrows shot to the top of her head. "I'm not having breakfast with you."

"Why not? All you've got is yogurt and fruit here. That's not going to do it for me."

"What does it for you isn't my concern." She put her hands on her small hips. "I let you stay here."

"Consider it a thank-you, then." He winked. "We'll discuss our future living arrangements. The couch is great but I'm going to need to get a bed."

She shook her head. "This is my apartment."

"Actually," he said slowly, "it's my sister-in-law's apartment. I have more rights to it than you."

Lexi's mouth dropped open and he found himself wanting to kiss it shut. "She's renting it to me."

"I don't like staying at the bar. I'm family." He grabbed her purse from the back of the chair and handed it to her. "My brother doesn't trust you after what you and your father tried to do."

She sucked in a breath.

"Don't make me use the family card."

"I'm ordering everything on the menu," she mumbled and headed out the door.

They drove in silence the few minutes to the restaurant. Scott could feel her frustration. He knew Julia didn't think much of him, and the truth was, his sister-in-law might very well rather rent her apartment to Lexi than him. He wasn't letting on, though.

He didn't want to stay at the bar. Although he would never admit it out loud, he didn't want to be by himself right now. He'd been living alone since he'd left home at eighteen. By nature, he was a loner. Even with girlfriends, he'd never been much of a stay-the-night snuggler. But he'd felt a strange sort of comfort knowing Lexi was sleeping down the hall last night. He had about a decade's worth of decent sleep to catch up on, and he was determined to make it happen.

She didn't order everything on the menu, but did ask for both an omelet and a stack of pancakes, plus granola on the side.

"Where do you put all that food?" he asked after their waitress had filled the table with plates. "You're no bigger than a minute and you've got enough calories on that plate for an NFL quarterback."

Reaching for the syrup, she answered, "It's going to be my dinner, too. I'll get a take-home box."

"So you conned me into buying you two meals?"

"I gave you a place to sleep last night." She took a big bite of pancake.

"Why do you need to hoard food? You don't strike me as someone hard up for money."

"I don't want to use my credit cards while I'm here." She stopped chewing midbite and stared at him, as if realizing she'd shared too much. "I'm trying to save money."

"You're hiding." He took a drink of coffee and studied her, the mystery that was his little pixie mouse falling into place. "From a boyfriend?"

She rolled her eyes. "No. My so-called boyfriend is probably relieved to get a break from me. My father set us up and I'm pretty sure he's only with me to improve his chances at making partner in the firm."

"Then he's an idiot." Scott held up a hand when she would have argued. "Don't change the subject. It must be your father. What happened between you and dear old dad?"

"Nothing," she muttered. "I just want some time on my own."

Scott shook his head. For an attorney, she was a terrible liar. "Tell me," he coaxed, extending his leg so he could brush against hers under the table. "Secrets are better when you share them."

She put down her fork. "It's not really a secret. I gave Julia some information about her ex-boyfriend's family that ensured they'd end the custody suit. They found out and dropped my father's firm. In turn, he dropped me."

"Not for good."

She shrugged. "From the moment I came to live with him, I've done everything he wanted me to. This is new ground for both of us."

"You're adopted?"

"When I was six. I'd been put into the foster system and shortly after, my mother died." Lexi drew in a breath and stared at her plate. "She was an alcoholic. I'd already been in two homes when my father found me. I owe him my life, really." When she looked up, tears shone in her big eyes. "But it's my life and I've never once made a decision just for me. He's mad now, but you're right, it's not forever. He's going to expect me to come back. Before I do, I need a little freedom. I'm going to see what it's like to do what I want to for a change."

"Why go back at all? If you want freedom, take it."

"It's not that simple."

"You're making it complex."

"I owe him."

"He's your father. That's not how it works with parents." Not that Scott had a lot of experience with unconditional love. His mother had died when he was a boy, killed in a car accident when she'd been driving after drinking. Her death had made his father pull away emotionally for years.

"When my father decided he wanted to adopt, he had fifteen kids in the foster system IQ tested. I happened to be the smartest of the bunch. That's how he picked me."

The thought made Scott cringe. "Is that even legal?"

"It doesn't matter. He made it happen." Lexi took a drink of juice, holding the tiny glass in front of her like a shield. "I always understood that I'd been given a great opportunity. And that I'd be a fool to jeopardize it. So I didn't. I was perfect, exactly who he wanted me to be. Up until seven months ago, I was more Stepford daughter than real person. I'm grateful for everything he did for me and I love him." She put down the juice and gestured with her hands. "This is all pretend to me. He made me the person I am and I can't change that. I'm going to take this time and enjoy it."

"Then what?" Scott almost didn't want to hear the answer.

She bit her bottom lip. "Then I go back to regular life. Or I go a different way. I need time to figure that out."

The waitress came to the table. "Could you box all

this up for us?" Scott asked, gesturing to the three plates still sitting in front of Lexi.

"Sure thing, sweetie." As she picked up the dishes, she smiled at him. "Aren't you the new owner over at Riley's?" she crooned.

He returned her grin. "Guilty as charged."

"I've always preferred Cowboys," she told him. Scott knew the other bar in town had loud country music, a huge dance floor and a mechanical bull. His version of hell. "But," she continued, leaning closer to him, "it might be worth a change of venue one of these nights."

"We'd love to see you over there."

Lexi cleared her throat and nudged the waitress's arm with one of the plates. "You forgot this."

She turned, as if noticing her for the first time. "Thanks," she muttered before walking away.

"I don't get why you're such a magnet for women." Lexi huffed out a breath. "What's so special about you?"

"Where do I begin?" he asked with a laugh, enjoying how bothered she was by the other woman's attention to him, even if he couldn't quite explain why. "But you're changing the subject again. You think by not using your credit cards, your father won't find you? What about when you use your cell phone?"

"I haven't yet." She fidgeted in her chair. "I don't expect you to understand. I need time, that's all."

He understood better than she knew. After everything he'd seen and done, if he could take a break from his messed-up life for a time, he'd gladly do it. Maybe that was why he'd made the impulsive offer to buy the bar in the first place. It was an expensive way to keep himself busy while he regrouped, but that was what he needed. After the incident, his superiors had wanted him to see a counselor while the internal investigation ran its course. According to his boss, it was standard when a marshal was killed in the line of duty and part of the requirement to have his administrative leave lifted.

Not that it mattered. Scott wasn't sure he'd ever go back. He still had the resignation letter he'd drafted. Any day now he'd get around to sending it.

He grabbed Lexi's hand as she made to stand from the table. "Not so fast. I bought you enough breakfast to feed a fire station. But we haven't talked about our living arrangement."

Lexi stared at him as a shiver ran down her spine. He couldn't be serious. "You can't live with me," she whispered.

"Why not?"

"People will talk about us."

"You think so?" he answered as the waitress came back to the table with a large bag of to-go cartons and the check.

She slid the small piece of paper toward Scott with a wink. "My phone number's on the back. When you get a night off, give me a call."

"How can she do that?" Lexi said with a hiss as the woman walked away again. "I'm sitting right here. It's like I'm invisible. For all she knows, we're on a date. We could have spent the night together and she's propositioning you while I watch."

"If I was staying at the apartment with you, maybe the flocks of women would back off." He wiggled his eyebrows.

Lexi did a mental eye roll, but at the same time her stomach fluttered. Scott Callahan was exactly the kind of man her father had warned her about for years. A bad boy to the core. Maybe that was part of the reason she found him so appealing.

She knew it was a bad idea, but said, "If I let you stay there, I don't want any more talk about me being fired."

He chuckled. "You're a terrible waitress. You know that, right?"

"*Terrible* is a strong word."

"You break more glasses than drinks you serve."

"I'm getting better," she argued.

"True, but you'll never be a natural."

"Those are my terms." She grabbed the bag of food and made her way toward the door.

Scott caught up to her easily as she rounded the street corner. "How long are you planning on staying here?" He grabbed her elbow and swung her around to face him.

She stared at him, not sure how to respond. "A month. Six weeks? However long it takes."

"I won't fire you for a month. You let me stay at the apartment for four weeks and I'll let you keep your job. Deal?"

She watched the fall breeze play with the waves of his hair. His hands were shoved in his pockets and he looked as if he didn't have a care in the world. His jeans hugged the strong muscles of his legs and his faded flannel shirt was unbuttoned enough to reveal a small patch of hair on his chest. Every part of him was the essence of cool.

But his eyes told her a different story. A tale of loneliness, loss and a need that called to her own secret, lonely heart.

"Okay," she said quickly, before she changed her mind. "I mean, since you're Julia's brother-in-law, she certainly wouldn't mind you crashing there, too."

He tried to hide the smile that played at the corner of his mouth. "You won't regret it."

"I already do," she muttered. "You need to get your own bed. By tonight."

He nodded. "I can do that."

"Would you really have fired me?"

His grin widened. "You'll never know. I have to be at the bar for some deliveries. I'll give you a lift back to your apartment first."

"I need to do some things in town, so I can walk back later. It's not far. I'll have an extra key made and leave it under the front mat." She lifted the bag. "Thanks for breakfast. And dinner."

She was brushing him off, but Scott didn't want to push the first good luck he'd had in ages. He reached forward and tapped his finger on the tip of her nose. "Have a good day, Lexi."

She pushed her hair behind her ears and watched him walk away. Her stomach gurgled and she hoped it was from the food rather than her reaction to Scott.

Halfway down the sidewalk, she noticed a light on in Julia's salon. The place was closed until noon, according to the sign in the window. But the front door was unlocked, so she let herself in. Closing the door behind her, she heard the patter of feet, then a dog was in front of her. He was big and gray and barked several times before showing his teeth.

Lexi pressed her back against the wall of windows at the front of the building. "Good doggie," she whispered.

The animal's lip curled back even more and she could have sworn he snarled at her. Lexi felt her recently eaten breakfast threaten to make a repeat appearance. At least that might distract the dog long enough for her to get away. She concentrated on breathing without passing out.

"Casper?"

Lexi heard Julia's voice from the back of the salon. "Julia," she called softly. The dog came a step closer to her. "It's Lexi. I, uh, your dog… Can you come…?"

"He's friendly." Julia walked toward her, hands on her hips.

"Really?" Lexi's voice was a high-pitched squeak. "Why is he snarling at me?"

"He smiles." The woman placed a hand on the dog's broad back. "Casper, sit."

He plopped to the ground.

"Pet him," Julia suggested. "He'll love you."

Lexi swallowed and held out a hand. She ran her palm along the animal's silky head. He immediately flipped on his back, wriggling in ecstasy as Lexi rubbed him with more enthusiasm. "He's a sweetie."

"Told you so."

"How well do you know Sam's brother?" Lexi asked, keeping her attention focused on the dog.

"Not very," Julia admitted. "He and Sam aren't close. They never have been. Has he been giving you trouble at the bar?"

Lexi shook her head, straightening. "He's been okay. It's just…weird, right? That he bought the bar and is staying in Brevia."

"There's more than one person in Brevia who doesn't belong right now."

Lexi felt herself blush. "I'm sorting things out. This is a little detour, that's all. Does it bother you that I'm here? I put a lot on you and maybe it didn't feel like you had a choice but to help." A thought crossed her mind. "I don't want to make it uncomfortable for you. Scott said Sam doesn't like me."

"Can you blame him?"

"No," Lexi admitted, cringing. She loved her work and the law, but hated some of the things she'd had to do as part of her job. Her father had so many powerful clients and Lexi had spent a lot of her time digging up dirt on their enemies, often people with a lot less money and influence. It made her feel like the stereotypical unethical attorney, and she wished it could be different.

"Actually, I like thinking I'm getting back at your dad in a way." Julia smiled at her. "Not that I'm vindictive or anything, but he and the Johnsons made my life difficult. You know what they say about payback." She absently straightened one of the styling bays. "Don't worry about Sam. He's protective of me. But it's all good."

Lexi noticed Julia's dreamy smile. "You're lucky to have someone who loves you like that."

"Agreed," Julia said. "How is the apartment? Other than the basics, I didn't leave a lot of stuff there."

"It's great. Thank you again. I get paid at the end of this week so I should be able to get you more than the deposit, but..."

"Don't worry about it," Julia told her. "I know you're good for it. It's not too weird in a strange place by yourself?"

Lexi thought about Scott sleeping on her couch and shook her head. "I'm fine." She should tell Julia about their new arrangement, but the words wouldn't form. "I noticed a few dog toys in the closet."

"I found Casper when I was living there." Julia bent

forward to scratch between the dog's ears. "Or I should say, he found me."

"So the building is pet friendly?"

The stylist studied her. "You don't seem like a dog person."

"I don't know," Lexi admitted. "My father never let me have pets. Dogs make me nervous." She gave a small laugh. "Almost everything makes me nervous. But this adventure is all about trying new things."

"An animal is a big commitment. It's not just something you try out for a little, then dump when you go back to your real life."

"I know that." Lexi's resolve suddenly got stronger. She'd never experienced unconditional love, but was sure she had it in her to give. She'd always wanted a pet, but had been afraid that even a dog or cat might not think she was good enough. She didn't know anything about caring for an animal. Suddenly, it was very important to prove it to herself. "What time does the animal shelter your mom runs open?"

Julia glanced at her watch. "Not for another hour. But I have an in with the owner, if you know what I mean."

"You don't have to help me with this. You've done more than enough already. I'm not here to take charity from you."

"I've got a good instinct for matching dogs with their forever people." Julia grabbed a leash off the hook on the wall. "But you can return the favor. One of the girls is going through a divorce and she's feeling uneasy about the filing. Frank Davis is her attorney, the same one I used. He's not giving her the time she needs. I'll take you out to the shelter, and in return, you look over the paperwork for her."

Lexi had run away from her life and her job, but she still loved the law. Maybe giving legal advice to someone here could start to make up for all the things she'd done as an attorney that weren't helpful.

She nodded, loving the sound of the word *forever*. She wanted to be a forever person, even if only to an animal. Plus, it would be good to have a distraction in the apartment when Scott was there.

"You've got yourself a deal."

Chapter Five

Scott arrived at the bar in the late afternoon, after spending the day in Charlotte buying more supplies and a mattress set to take to the apartment. At this rate, he was going to run through his savings within the month.

He was tired and, strangely, wanted to return to Lexi's. The two-bedroom apartment was nothing special and not nearly as stylish or comfortable as his condo in D.C., but he felt more at home there than anyplace he'd been in years.

He had work to do at the bar first. As soon as he walked into the building, the smell of spices and roasting…something…hit him. He followed his nose to the kitchen and found Jon Riley at the stove with four men sitting around the small table in the corner.

"Hey, there," he called to the group.

All four men jumped up, turning toward him with

varying degrees of mistrust in their eyes. "He invited us," one of them offered.

"We're allowed to be here," another insisted.

"Who are you, anyway?" a third asked.

Jon turned from the stove. "It's okay, guys." He motioned them to sit back down. "This is Scott Callahan, the bar's new owner. I told you about him. He's cool."

Scott didn't feel particularly cool at the moment. "Uh, Jon? What the hell is going on here?"

"I'm making an early dinner."

"You asked if you could use the kitchen to make yourself food. You forgot to mention company."

Jon turned the heat down on one of the burners and pointed to the hall. With a wary glance at the strangers sitting at the table, Scott turned and followed him there.

"I won't make a habit of it," he said with a shrug. "But these guys are like me. They don't have much and they've given a helluva lot more to this country than they've gotten back."

"They're ex-military?"

Joe nodded. "They need a break and a decent meal. I didn't think you'd be here this early. Thought I could get them fed and out before anyone noticed." He gave Scott a sheepish smile. "Sorry."

Scott scrubbed his hand across his face. His life was so far from the norm, he didn't know which way was up anymore. He was used to action, a mission and constantly moving. He was used to being on his own. Now he'd gotten himself a roommate and had a kitchen full of hungry men waiting for a meal. He shook his head. "Do you have enough for one more?"

Jon's grin looked out of place on his somber face. "You bet."

Scott walked back into the kitchen and sat down with the men, feeling an odd camaraderie with this misfit band of soldiers. They asked him a few questions about his military career, but mainly enjoyed the meal in a companionable silence he could appreciate. Then he took his first bite from the plate Jon placed in front of him and could barely stop himself from moaning out loud. He looked around at the other men, whose faces reflected the same food rapture he felt.

He met Jon's gaze. "This is beyond amazing," he said, then took another large bite. "I'm talking four-star-restaurant good."

"It's only a chicken potpie," Jon said with a shrug. "I like simple food that tastes good."

"It's a little bit of heaven," Scott agreed.

One of the men shook his fork at Jon. "Everything he makes is like this. I look forward to my weekly Jon fix like I used to crave the bottle."

"That's quite a comparison," Scott said with an uncomfortable laugh.

"Denny is in my AA group," Jon explained. "Like I said, I worked as a chef in New York, but the big-city lifestyle didn't exactly agree with me."

"Didn't you say Riley's used to serve food?" Scott asked.

He nodded. "It's where I got my start."

Scott looked around the large kitchen. "What would you think about putting together a menu?"

"Are you serious?"

"Nothing fancy, but a step up from normal bar food. Like you said, simple food that tastes good. If we could tap into part of the lunch and dinner crowd, it would expand the bar's reach in a great way. Riley's Bar & Grill. What do you think?"

"I think it's the best offer I've had in years," he answered, his voice thick.

A round of applause and several catcalls went up from the men.

Scott felt a smile spread across his face. He stood, shook hands with Jon, then grabbed his plate. "I'm glad you agree. Get something to me by end of day tomorrow. I'd like to get the new menu implemented by early next week."

"Will do, boss."

"I've got to put away some boxes out front, so I'm going to take my dinner to go." He turned to the men. "It was nice meeting you guys." He paused, then added, "If any of you are looking for work, let me know. There's a lot of odd jobs to be done around here, painting and the like."

"There aren't a lot of opportunities for guys like us," Denny answered. A couple of the men nodded in agreement. "Some of us got arrest records, pasts we're not too proud of."

"I know all about that," Scott answered. He pointed to Jon. "If he vouches for you, that's enough for me."

"Thanks, Mr. Callahan." Denny stepped forward and shook his hand. "You're a good man."

Scott smiled. "I don't know about that, but I'm a man in need of good help. Come in tomorrow morning and we'll talk work."

He finished the meal as he unloaded bottles into the cooler. He walked from the back with more beer and heard the front door open. Annoyance crept up his spine at his hope to see Lexi, who was on the schedule tonight, coming in early. He knew his interest in her would lead nowhere for either of them, but couldn't put a stop to it. Instead, his father and Sam stood inside the entrance.

"To what do I owe the honor?" he asked, setting the box on top of the bar.

"Scotty, it's so good to see you." His dad came forward and wrapped Scott in a tight hug, ignoring the way he stiffened in response. Joe Callahan had been the consummate Boston cop for years, both before and after his wife died. He'd dedicated his life to the force, even when he'd had two young sons at home grieving the loss of their mother. Joe's ability to cut off his feelings had been ingrained early in both his boys, which was just fine by Scott. Recently Joe had rediscovered his "emotional intelligence" as he called it, and was on a mission to make sure Sam and Scott came along for the ride.

Joe had traveled south last spring to reconnect with Sam, and in the process had gotten a second chance at love—with Julia's mother, Vera. Now both Sam and Joe called Brevia, North Carolina, home. Scott was happy for them, but he had no desire to be part of Joe's lovefest. He thought Sam had gone soft, and although he liked Julia and her little boy well enough, the thought of being tied down with a wife and kid felt totally foreign to him.

"Good to see you, old man. Married life is treating you well so far." He pulled back from Joe's tight hug. "Jeez, Dad, what's up with the tears?"

Joe swiped a hand across his face. "I'm happy to see you, son. Nothing wrong with showing my emotions."

"He's a regular watering pot," Sam added, clapping a hand on their dad's broad back. "How's it going here?"

"Coming along," Scott answered, stepping behind

the bar and out of Joe's reach. "Is this a social call or something else?"

"I've got a buddy who's a local Realtor specializing in commercial property," Sam said. "I can make a call and get him over here within fifteen minutes."

"Why do I need a Realtor?"

Sam exchanged a look with their father. "We thought he could help."

Scott pointed a finger at Joe. "You're in on this, too?"

"I want you to be happy, Scotty." He stepped forward. "You've been through a lot. You deserve it."

"It was an impulsive decision to buy this place," Sam said. "We get that. But Mark can help you unload it before things go too far."

"You think you know me so well," Scott muttered, transferring beer bottles into the cooler behind the bar.

"I know you love being a marshal, the action and adrenaline of it," his brother countered. "I know life as a bar owner can't give you that."

"I thought the same thing when you left the force in Boston to take the police chief's job in this Podunk Smoky Mountain town. It's worked out all right for you. Why not me?"

Sam shook his head, but Joe stepped between them. "Is this what you want, Scott? This kind of life change? Because I'll support whatever you want to do, whether it's going back to D.C. or staying in Brevia. Hell, I'll wipe bar tables for you if it would help."

"Dad, he's not staying in Brevia."

Scott felt his temper flare. Why didn't anyone around him think he could stick? "Is it so hard to believe I could make a life here in your precious town? I get that you don't want me here."

"It's not that, although could you blame me if it was?" Sam let out a breath. "The last time we were living in the same place, you slept with my fiancée. That's a hell of a breach of trust."

"You know why that happened. She'd already cheated on you and you wouldn't believe it. I had to prove it to you."

"By going after her yourself? That's not my definition of brotherly love."

Scott squeezed shut his eyes to ward off the dull pounding inside his head. When he opened them again, he saw Lexi standing just inside the front door. By the look on her face, she'd heard his conversation with Sam and the awful thing he'd done. He'd wanted to protect his brother, but ended up betraying him in the worst way possible. Sam was right—he'd made a huge alcohol-induced mistake when he'd taken Sam's former fiancée, Jenny, to bed.

Buying the bar had also been impulsive and alcohol-induced. Whether it was a mistake remained to be seen. Sam certainly thought it was, and probably their dad, as well. Scott met Lexi's gaze, surprise in her eyes, but not the judgment he'd come to expect from everyone around him. Maybe that would appear later. He couldn't say. But the absence of it bolstered his resolve.

He turned to face his brother and father. "I messed up, Sam. Royally. I'm sorry for what I did, but you have to believe that my intentions were good. Or don't believe it. It doesn't matter anymore. I'm here now and I'm staying in Brevia until I decide it's time to go. I'm not going to make a mess of the bar. I won't embarrass you in front of your wife or your neighbors. You have a life here. I get that."

He expected Sam to argue, but instead his brother gave a curt nod.

Joe put one arm around Sam's stiff shoulders and reached for Scott, hugging both men to his chest. "All three of us together again. I couldn't ask for anything more." He gave a loud sniff and Scott saw Sam roll his eyes. At least they were in agreement in not liking their father's emotional mumbo jumbo. "We should celebrate."

Scott looked over his father's shoulder to Lexi, who was gesturing wildly. He nodded as her meaning became clear. "We should celebrate the fact that both of you bozos were dumb enough to get caught in the marriage net. I'll throw a party here for you—a joint reception with all your friends. As big as you want it to be."

Sam shook his head. "I don't think so."

"It's a great idea." Joe clapped Scott on the back. "When are you thinking?"

"I need a few weeks to get everything running the way I want. How about a month from Saturday?"

"Perfect," Joe answered.

"No way," Sam said. "Julia won't agree to it."

"Nonsense," Joe argued. "Vera will be thrilled and Julia will agree to anything that makes her mother happy."

"I'm sure you want to make your mother-in-law slash new stepmother happy, Sammy-boy."

Joe nodded. "If Vera's happy, we're all happy."

Scott got a good bit of satisfaction in watching his brother's jaw clench. "Why are you doing this?" Sam asked.

How did he answer that? Because his old life held too many reminders of the partner he'd lost. Because he couldn't stand to be alone anymore. Because he had to keep moving, stay busy to keep the demons at bay. His chest tightened but he held Sam's gaze. "I want to make things right between us. At least let me try."

"Fine." Sam looked over his shoulder at Lexi, then back at him. "I thought you were going to fire her."

Scott felt that unfamiliar surge of protectiveness wash over him again. "Leave her alone, Sam. We've come to an understanding."

"She's trouble and I don't trust her."

Scott watched Lexi walk forward until she stood directly behind Sam. Scott had a couple of inches on his brother, but Sam was broader, making Lexi look even tinier so close to him. "I can hear you talking about me," she told Sam.

"I don't particularly care," he said, glancing at her again.

"Do you work here with Scotty?" Joe asked, oblivious to the tension between Sam and Lexi. "I'm Joe Callahan, his proud father."

Proud father? Scott groaned. Next Joe would be handing out cigars to customers, as if Scott's being in Brevia was cause for a real celebration. It was too bad his dad hadn't been around like this when he was a kid. Joe had been a workaholic cop, leaving the raising of his two young sons mostly to their mother, so he could put his life on the line for the force. And after Scott's mom died, things had gotten even worse, with Joe working extra shifts so he could bury the pain of his loss. Unfortunately, Scott had been stuck with his own pain and loss, but too young to know how to deal with them. Maybe things would have turned out differently if his mom was still around, but he'd never know. All he had was the present moment. "Dad, this is Lexi Preston. She's one of the waitresses here."

"Nice to meet you, Mr. Callahan."

"Call me Joe." He took her hand and brushed his lips across her knuckles. "If all the waitresses are as pretty as you, this place should do a bang-up business."

"Dad, inappropriate." Scott felt his jaw drop as Lexi giggled. He hadn't heard her laugh before. The sweet sound washed over him and made him crave more.

"I don't mind," she said, tipping her chin down as a blush crept up her cheeks.

Scott sucked in a breath as she smoothed her hands across the fabric of her dark miniskirt.

Sam nudged him. "Be careful, little brother. I still don't trust her."

Joe turned to Sam, frowning. "You're being rude, Sammy. I didn't raise you to disrespect a lady like that."

"It's true, Dad."

"Thanks for the compliment, Joe." Lexi met Sam's angry stare and swallowed. "But your son has good reason to mistrust me. I worked on the custody case against Julia Morgan. I put her and Sam through a lot and I'm sorry for that."

Joe crossed his arms over his chest. "Is that so?"

"I also gave Julia the information that helped her get the lawsuit dropped, if that makes a difference." She glanced toward the front of the bar as if she wanted to bolt, then turned back to the three men. "I know I have to earn your trust, and I'm going to do that, Sam. Julia has given me a chance and I'm very grateful to her."

"A chance at what?" Joe asked.

"A chance for a fresh start." Lexi took a deep breath. "I'm going to live by my terms and that means helping people instead of hurting them. I learned a lot in the past couple of months. I've gotten a second chance and I'm going to make the most of it."

Joe studied her with his best hard-nosed cop stare. Scott knew the look well, as he and his trouble-making buddies had caved under it many times growing up. Lexi didn't look away and Scott realized that his little mouse had a lot more backbone than he'd given her credit for. Suddenly, Joe reached out a hand and pulled Lexi into one of his trademark bear hugs.

"You've got to be kidding me," Sam muttered under his breath.

"It takes a lot of guts to admit you've made a mistake. I'm proud of you, Lexi. We'll be here to help you every step of the way."

Joe released Lexi and she stepped back, looking a little dazed, much like Scott felt. "That means a lot, Joe." She quickly swiped at her cheeks and kept her eyes to the ground. "I've got to clock in now. I'll, um… Thank you."

With that, she raced through the door that led to the back of the bar.

Scott wanted to follow her, but turned to his father. "What was that, Dad? You made her cry."

"When are you going to learn there's nothing wrong with tears?"

"Excuse me, but you were the one who told me to man up after Mom died. I was seven, and as I remember, there was a strict no-tears rule."

Joe wiped at his own eyes. "I'm sorry, boys. I know I made big mistakes. But we're all together now and things are going to be back on track with the three of us." He pulled Scott to him and let out a shuddering breath.

"Okay, Dad, sure." Scott looked at Sam. "Is he always like this now?"

"Yep. Welcome to Joe Callahan 2.0." Sam nudged their father. "Come on, old man. Scott has work to do."

"I'll have Vera call you about the details of the reception. She'll be thrilled."

Scott's eyes widened at the thought of dealing with his spirited new stepmother. For the first time today, Sam smiled. "Be careful what you wish for," he cautioned, then turned for the front door.

Joe stopped and looked back at Scott. "Do you have a place yet? You're welcome to stay with Vera and me."

"I'm set. Thanks, though."

Sam's eyes narrowed, but Scott ignored him. "See you, boys," he called, then turned back to his cases of beer.

Lexi entered another order into the computer and turned away from the bar as a hand clamped down on her wrist.

"You're avoiding me," Scott said, leaning toward her.

"I'm hustling so you don't have a reason to complain about me."

"I wasn't aware I needed a reason."

"Don't you have bottles to open?" She blew a strand of hair out of her eyes, then stilled as he brushed his thumb across her face.

"I'm an excellent multitasker," he said, somehow making the words sound like foreplay.

She shrugged out of his grasp and stepped away from the bar, his quiet laugh flustering her even more. She still hadn't recovered from the emotions that had bubbled to the surface when Joe Callahan said he was proud of her.

Never once since she'd been adopted had her own father said anything like that to her, despite the fact that she'd made it her life's mission to make him proud. Instead, the more she'd tried, the more he seemed to expect, until she felt more like a machine than a real person. Now, by her simply admitting she wanted to do better, Scott's dad had given her the validation she craved. How weak and pathetic did that make her?

She was totally off-balance, which may have explained why, when Jon poked his head out of the back of the bar and told her she had an emergency call, she automatically took the cordless phone and held it to her ear.

"Hello," she said into the receiver.

"Lexi." Her father spoke her name like an admonishment. It was a tone she recognized all too well.

She sucked in a breath. "How did you find me?"

"The better question is why are you hiding from me?"

"I'm not hiding," she said softly, holding the phone close to her ear to hear over the background noise in the bar. Although it was a weekday night, a decent crowd had trickled in to watch the evening's game on the big screen. "You fired me. I left. That's how it works."

"No need to be snippy, Lexi," her father said, his voice clipped. "I acted in a moment of anger. I think your leave of absence has gone on long enough. I'll expect to see you at the office Monday morning."

Lexi bit down on her lip until she could swear she tasted blood. She'd known this was going to happen, that her father would reel her back in eventually. She was too valuable a commodity for him to truly let her go. But she'd hoped to have more time. "I'm not ready."

"Excuse me?"

"I want to stay," she said, trying to give her voice a confidence she didn't feel.

"To spend your nights in a bar in that backwoods Southern town? I don't think so. With your biological history, that's a very bad idea. I'll see you Monday and—"

"No!"

Silence greeted her outburst. "I'm taking a month. I have the personal days." She spoke quickly so as not to lose her nerve. "I'll let you know then if and when I'm coming back. Goodbye, Daddy."

With trembling fingers, she clicked off the receiver and held it tight against her chest, her stomach turning. She'd never disobeyed her father before. Yes, she was twenty-seven years old, but when it came to her relationship with Robert Preston, she felt more like a schoolgirl, afraid of his dissatisfaction, disappointment and ultimately his rejection. Her biggest fear was that the man who'd rescued her from her awful childhood would leave her with nothing and no one in her life. She knew he had the power to do that, at least as far as her career went. Still, she couldn't give up now. She needed to know she could make it on her own if she had hope of going back to her old life with any shred of dignity intact.

She felt someone watching her and looked up to see Scott standing stock-still next to the bar, the waitresses a flurry of activity around him. Lexi tried to throw him a casual smile, but her mouth wouldn't move in that direction so she fled to the back of the bar. With a calming breath, she headed into his small office at the end of the hall and returned the phone to its cradle. Scrubbing her hands across her face, she turned and ran smack into Scott's rock wall of a chest.

"Who was on the phone?" he asked, holding her upper arms to steady her.

"It was personal. None of your business."

"You look like someone called to say they'd shot your puppy."

"That's awful." She tried to step way, but he held her in place, one finger tracing small circles on her skin, as if he was trying to soothe her. She hated to admit that it worked, but felt herself sagging a bit, the conversation with her father draining what little energy she had left from the day.

"I'm guessing you got the call from dear old dad?" Scott asked softly.

She nodded. "I blocked the firm's and his personal numbers from my cell and haven't been picking up callers I don't recognize. It was sneaky of him, phoning the bar."

"He's an attorney—what do you expect?"

"Lawyer jokes. Funny." But she smiled a little. "He wants me in the office on Monday."

Scott's fingers stilled on her arm, which made her glance up into his suddenly unreadable eyes. "Are you going?"

"No. Not yet, anyway. I like it here, the apartment, the small town." She gave a tiny laugh. "Even this crummy job. The boss is a jerk but the customers are great."

"Boss jokes. Funny." One side of his mouth kicked up before drawing into a tight line. "Will your father come looking for you?"

"I don't think so. I told him I needed a month."

"What happens in a month?"

"I'm not sure, but it gives me time to figure it out."

"You can take care of yourself, you know. You had

my dad eating out of the palm of your hand minutes after you told him you'd tried to take his grandson away."

"Your dad's a big teddy bear."

Scott grinned. "I've never thought of him that way."

His smile disarmed her, made her breath hitch. She wanted him in a way she couldn't explain and barely understood. Clearly, she wasn't his type, and he was way too much…man for her. But it didn't stop her body's response to him. He met her gaze, and the way his blue eyes darkened made her think he might feel the same. She knew her time in Brevia would eventually come to an end, and she wanted to experience everything she could while she was here. Maybe that was what made her blurt, "Have an affair with me?"

Scott's grip on her arm loosened. His fists clenched and she thought he might walk away. "You can't want that."

"I do." She licked her lip and felt the electricity of desire charge between them. "More than you know."

His hands smoothed up her arms and across her shoulders to her neck, his fingers burning a path along her heated skin. He cradled her head in his hands as one thumb traced the seam of her lips. "You should be gentler with this mouth," he told her, soothing the spot she'd bit down on earlier. "I've grown to like it quite a lot."

She could hardly manage a breath, but whispered, "What if gentle isn't what I want?"

He cupped her face, tilting her chin up and leaning in so they were so close she could smell the peppermint scent of his breath. "You don't know what you're asking, Lexi."

"Show me."

Heaven help her, he did. His mouth covered hers, igniting a fire in her belly that quickly spread out of control. Which was exactly what she wanted: to lose control with this man. Right here, right now. As his lips teased hers, she lifted her arms around his neck, pressing her body against him.

Scott groaned low in his throat and deepened the kiss, his mouth making demands that she tried her best to meet. His hands moved down, just brushing the outline of her breasts, making her gasp. He took the opportunity to tangle his tongue with hers and she lost all coherent thought, so caught up in the physical sensations that were flooding through her.

When he pulled back she thought she might melt into a puddle on the floor, that was how boneless and weightless he'd made her feel. "Don't stop," she said, reaching for him again.

"No."

That one word brought her back to reality like a swift kick to her stomach. She blinked several times to clear her head. "You don't mean that. The way you were just kissing me, you can't mean that."

He shook his head, his hands clenched at his sides. "You're not thinking clearly and you want to get back at your father. I understand that. But I'm not going to take advantage of your weakness."

"I'm not weak."

"I didn't mean—"

"I get to make my own decisions." She adjusted her shirt where it had bunched around her waist, embarrassed that she was still reeling from the kiss, when Scott could clearly pull away with no problem. "Good or bad, the point of me being on my own is to live on my own terms."

"Which involve a relationship with me?"

She crossed her arms over her chest. "Not a relationship. An affair. You know…"

"Sex?" he offered.

"Well…yes. Casual. Fun. Easy. All things that have been missing from my life since…forever, really."

"You don't strike me as the casual-sex type."

"That's the point." She wanted to stomp her foot in frustration. Why was he making this so complicated? Couldn't he just go back to kissing her and see where that led?

"My answer is still no," he said quietly.

Tears of embarrassment clogged her throat. Here she was, all but throwing herself at his feet, only to be rejected. "Because I'm not your type."

"Because of a lot of reasons. I don't—"

"It's fine." She held up a hand. "There's no need to go on. We both need to get back to work."

He shook his head as he watched her. "It's a slow night. Take the rest of it off. You look like you could use it."

Lexi felt a blush burn her cheeks. He was going to reject her, then tell her she looked like hell? Great. Insult to injury, why would she expect anything else?

"What I need," she said, straightening her shoulders and setting her jaw so he wouldn't see how his words stung, "is a drink. It works for you. Why not me? I'm going to have an adventure with or without you, Scott. Just wait and see." Mustering every ounce of dignity she could grasp, she walked past him back toward the bar.

Chapter Six

Scott put his key in the lock, then leaned forward to listen for any sound coming from the apartment. It was late, past 2:00 a.m., and thankfully, things seemed to be quiet here. He wasn't sure if he could keep his temper at Lexi's ridiculous proposition, not to mention his desire for her, in check if she was still awake.

He wasn't sure how things had gone bad so quickly. Not that they'd ever been particularly good between them, but he'd thought they'd reached an understanding. Then he'd seen her take that phone call, shock and misery evident on her face. He'd known it was a mistake to follow her back to his office, but he'd had to make sure she was okay. She wasn't, and after minutes spent kissing her, neither was he. Holding a woman in his arms had never affected him the way being with Lexi had.

When she'd made the offer of an affair, parts of his

body had literally jumped to attention. But he couldn't agree to it. He had a track record of hurting the people he cared about, and although he'd known her only a short time, he felt an undeniable connection to Lexi. Whether it was his mother or Sam or his late partner at the Marshals, Derek, Scott's need and desire to protect them turned to poison.

It had become easier to keep people at arm's length. He'd also become an expert at avoiding the pain of rejection or having someone he cared about not believing him. Lexi was a good person, pure of heart in a way he could never hope to be. For once he was going to do the right thing, even if it killed him.

It just might, he thought as the door opened to reveal Lexi asleep on the couch in nothing but a tank top and boxer shorts. Her legs curled under her, the skin creamy all the way down to her bright red toenail polish. Legs he could well imagine wrapped around him.

A low sound coming from the other side of the couch distracted him. A moment later there was a flash of brown fur accompanied by several high, yippy barks, and a small dog sunk its teeth into the toe of Scott's work boot.

"What the—" He shook his foot but the tiny dog had clamped on tight.

Lexi sat up, rubbing her eyes. "What's going on? What time is it?"

She wiped a hand across her mouth and Scott was momentarily distracted from the dog attack by the fact that Lexi wasn't wearing a bra. Was she trying to kill him?

The small animal holding tight to his boot was certainly intent on the job.

Lexi's sleepy gaze met Scott's, then dropped to his

leg. "Oh, no. Freddy, no. Come here, sweetheart." She moved around the side of the sofa, then dropped to her knees on the carpet. "Come, Freddy," she said, and with one last growl, the small pup jumped into her arms.

Scott closed the door behind him and contemplated the picture of Lexi on her knees in front of him. The couch in his office at the bar was suddenly looking more appealing.

"What is that thing?" he asked, dropping his keys on the table next to the door. He went to take a step into the apartment, but the dog turned and barked.

"It's not a thing. It's a dog. He's my dog." She picked him up as she stood, the small animal licking her chin with its pink tongue. "His name is Freddy."

Scott shook his head. "That's not a dog. You could make a case for an overgrown rat, or a football with legs, but it's definitely not a dog."

Lexi cradled the animal close to her chest, covering its ears at the same time. "Don't say things like that. He has a bit of a Napoleon complex. You're going to make it worse."

Scott couldn't imagine this night getting much worse. "Where did he come from?"

"The Morgans' animal shelter, of course. Julia helped me pick him out. Freddy and I bonded right away. He's a Chihuahua mix."

"Mixed with rodent I'd bet." All Scott wanted was to go to sleep, and now he couldn't get past the apartment's entrance without mini-Cujo gunning for him.

"Scott, please. My father never let me have a pet, not even a goldfish. I love Freddy. He needs me." Lexi's voice was a plea. "He's obviously a good watchdog.

That's important when you're a single woman living alone."

"You don't live alone. I live here, too."

She tilted her head. "You never know what I might need protection from."

That was the truth if he'd ever heard it, especially with one thin strap of her tank top sliding down the smooth skin of her upper arm. He refocused his attention on the dog. "He's going to have to get used to me."

"Come sit down on the couch with us."

Areas low in Scott's body tightened. The last thing he needed was to be sitting close to Lexi on the soft couch. "I'm tired. I want to go to sleep."

"In a minute," she argued and reached for his hand, lacing her fingers through his. "I want you to see how sweet Freddy is."

Her smile, both excited and tentative, did Scott in. There was nothing he could do to resist her.

She led him to the sofa, Freddy still nestled in her arms, and they sat side by side, the length of her bare leg pressed against his thigh. Even with his jeans between them, he could sense how soft her skin was. Knew it would feel like silk against his hands, his mouth. With a shake of his head, he looked at her holding the dog. "What do you want me to do?"

"Don't move," she answered. "I'm going to let him go so he can check you out. Don't make eye contact with him."

"Seriously?"

"Julia's mom told me that's how you start when a dog is nervous." Lexi smiled at Scott again. "Just close your eyes."

"Can I fall asleep?"

"No, but close your eyes."

He sighed and did as she asked, letting his head fall back. Despite how tired he was, there was no chance of him falling asleep sitting this close to Lexi. She smelled like heaven, and as she spoke softly to the dog, Scott imagined her soothing words were for him. That was until she let go of the animal, who promptly stepped into the middle of his lap. Scott let out a grunt of pain and the dog growled.

"Don't move," Lexi commanded, using her hand to push Scott against the cushions once more. "You'll spook him."

"If he bites me, all bets are off."

"He's not going to bite you, but don't open your eyes yet."

Her arm pressed into his shoulder as she spoke to the dog. "Good boy, Freddy. You make friends."

Scott felt a wet dog nose press against his neck. "That tickles," he whispered.

"Don't be a baby," Lexi answered.

"Me or the dog?"

"You, of course. Oh, look at that."

He opened his eyes just as the dog curled into a ball on his lap. Scott's gaze lifted to Lexi, her head tipped forward so close all he had to do was move the tiniest inch to taste her again. He craved her more than he'd ever wanted a drink. More than he could remember wanting anything.

"They say dogs are a good judge of character," she whispered. "Freddy likes you."

"I still think Freddy is more rat than dog."

"Don't be mean. I love him."

"You've had him less than a day."

"It only takes a moment to fall in love."

Scott's mouth went dry. He could say with certainty he'd never been in love. After his mother's death, he hadn't wanted to feel the pain of losing someone he loved again. Sitting here on the couch with Lexi, he could imagine what it would feel like to be in love, to truly let another person in. The crazy part was he'd bet it would feel a lot like the pitch in his heart right now.

Needing to bring the conversation back to a safer subject, he said, "I saw you talking to a few different guys tonight at the bar."

He'd wanted to engage her temper, but she smiled at him instead. "I know. I flirted a ton."

Scott tried not to groan. "Do you think that's a good idea? You don't want to give them the wrong impression."

"I do, though." Her smile grew wider. "Not give the wrong impression," she added quickly. "I want to meet new people, try new things. Flirting is one of them."

"Heaven help the men of Brevia."

She swatted his arm. "One of them asked me out, you know."

The hand Scott was using to pet Freddy clenched into a fist. "Who asked you out?"

"I doubt you know him. His name's Mark. He's a teacher at the high school." Lexi's eyes dropped to Scott's mouth and awareness traced a long path down his spine. "He seemed nice enough."

Nice. Lexi deserved *nice,* a word that had never been in Scott's vocabulary. He thought of her pressed against him in his office earlier, how open and responsive she'd been and how much it had affected him. Would she melt against Mark the same way?

The thought made Scott crazy. He wanted to pull her to him now, brand her as his so she was ruined for anyone else.

But that wasn't his right, because he had nothing to offer her and they both knew it.

The dog stirred on his lap, a welcome distraction. "Do you have a leash?" Scott asked.

"On the counter."

"Go to bed, Lexi. I'll take the rat out one more time to do his business." He lifted Freddy off his lap, tucking him under one arm. He grabbed the leash from the kitchen.

Lexi stood next to the sofa, arms crossed over her chest. "You're okay with me going on a date?" Her voice was strained.

"It's your life, sweetheart," he answered, not adding how much he wanted to be a part of it. He clipped the dog's collar to the leash and headed out the door.

Lexi walked along the path around the park, Freddy trotting ahead of her. She'd taken to morning walks during the past week to make sure she had as little to do with Scott as possible. Of course, she still saw him every night at the bar, but other than putting in orders, she had almost no contact with him.

She hated to admit how embarrassed she was about her behavior, practically begging him to sleep with her, only to have him reject her. And when she'd told him she was going on a date with another guy, the stupid, girlie part of her had hoped to make Scott jealous. Relieved was more like it, she realized now.

She was so busy wallowing in self-pity she didn't

notice someone walk up behind her until she felt a tap
on her shoulder.

"You look a million miles away," Julia said, handing
Lexi a steaming to-go mug.

"Kind of…. What's this for?" Lexi took the cup,
watching as Julia bent down to scratch between Freddy's perky ears.

"I've seen you the past couple of mornings, walking around the park like the hounds of hell are nipping
your heels. I thought you could use someone to talk to."

Lexi made a face. "It's supposed to look like I'm out
for exercise."

"Sam told me you let Scott move into the apartment."

"It's hard to believe anyone has the power to let that
man do anything." Lexi took a sip of the hot tea and
sighed. "But, yes, he's there with me. I didn't think you'd
mind. It's okay, isn't it?"

"Of course. How's that going?"

"I've been in the park every morning. Do I need to
say more?"

"I'll take a lap with you." Julia began walking in the
same direction as Lexi. "I also heard you were at Cowboys last night."

"Word travels fast," Lexi muttered.

"Welcome to a small town." Julia sighed.

"It was my night off."

"And you decided to spend it in the only other bar in
town? That doesn't seem like you."

"You don't know me very well."

Lexi tried to make her tone sound dismissive, but
Julia only laughed. "I also heard you were putting the
moves on several different guys."

"What the…? Are you having me followed now? As

thankful as I am for your help, it's none of your business what I do with my time, Julia." Lexi looked down at the ground, cursing the blush she felt rising to her cheeks.

"I know. And I know you're here to taste freedom, have a grand adventure, whatever. But I can tell you from personal experience that once you get a reputation, it can stick for a long time."

Lexi stopped to untangle Freddy's leash. The dog nuzzled against her legs and tears sprang to her eyes. "It's a lot of work, being totally on your own." She wiped at her cheek and looked at Julia. "I really admire you for taking care of yourself the way you did."

As part of the custody suit, it had been Lexi's job to delve into Julia's past, trying to dig up dirt that could be used against her. There had been a fair bit of it, mostly stemming from bad decisions Julia had made while trying to hide the learning disability that plagued her most of her life. But Julia was strong and kept fighting. In the process of her investigation, Lexi had come to respect her and understand that there were choices in life beyond doing what people expected of you. Once Julia had started living life on her terms, things had worked out for her. Lexi only hoped she could have an ounce of the woman's personal success.

"You're doing a fine job of taking care of yourself, Lexi." Julia smiled at her. "But you can't hold your alcohol."

Lexi snorted. "I know. But I don't have friends other than the girls at the bar. I didn't want to be alone in the apartment on my night off. That seemed too pathetic."

"There's nothing wrong with being alone if the alternative is hanging out with the wrong people."

They started walking again when Freddy tugged on

the leash. "My stylist, Nancy, said you were a big help to her with her divorce case."

"It's not my area of expertise," Lexi said with a shrug, "but her case is pretty cut-and-dried. I'm not sure why Frank Davis couldn't be of more help to her."

"Frank's been Brevia's main attorney for decades now. I think he might be slipping a bit. People are waiting for him to retire or at least bring in a junior associate, but he hasn't done it yet."

"I know from my dad there can be a lot of pride of ownership in having your own practice."

"People still need lawyers. Good ones." Julia pointed her coffee cup toward Lexi. "Like you."

"I'm not practicing law in Brevia."

"But you're certified in North Carolina?"

Lexi hesitated, then said, "I'm taking a break."

"Right. For the grand adventure." They'd done a full turn of the park and Julia stopped at the same place she'd met up with Lexi. "I have another friend who could use some legal counsel. Or at least a second opinion."

Lexi shook her head. "Grand adventure, remember?"

"She's a longtime client and needs help with an estate inheritance."

"Not my area of expertise, either."

"Please. It's a bad situation. She needs someone she can trust. We both know how that feels." Julia raised her eyebrows. "Don't make me beg, Lexi. It's not in my nature."

Lexi threw her cup into a nearby trash can. "Fine. Give her my cell number, but I'd like to go to that attorney's office and give him a piece of my mind."

"I'd like to see that." Julia tipped her cup in Lexi's

direction. "By the way, I'm having a girls' night in the salon tomorrow night. Are you off?"

"I can get off." Lexi fiddled with the leash, trying not to show too obviously her excitement at being included. "Are you sure? You don't have to ask me just to be nice."

Julia threw her head back and laughed. "Everyone knows I don't do anything to be nice. Some *nice* girls work at the salon, though. A couple of them are new to town. It would be a better place than a meat-market country bar to make friends."

"Great, then," Lexi said with a grin. "Thank you." She paused, then added, "I have a date."

"With Scott?"

Lexi ignored the wave of disappointment that rushed over her. "No. His name is Mark Childs. He's a teacher at the high school. He moved up from Charlotte last year. He's nice, too." She took a breath. "Sorry, I'm babbling."

"I'm glad for you. That sounds like a good addition to the adventure." To her surprise, Julia leaned forward and gave her a quick hug. "See you tomorrow, then."

"Okay, I'll see you." Lexi turned away quickly, surprised as well that her throat was suddenly a bit scratchy. But she felt better about her life. Funny how one quick conversation could do that. She leaned forward to pet Freddy, who flopped onto his back, always glad to have more attention. After a minute, when she had her emotions in check once more, she headed down the path and toward home.

"Don't even think about taking advantage of that girl."

Scott looked up from the new bar menu at the woman standing, hands on hips, just inside the front door.

Jon Riley stood quickly. "I'll be in the back, boss. Call me when you're through here." In a quieter voice he added, "Or when she's through with you."

"Chicken," Scott muttered as Jon made his escape, clucking over his shoulder.

"To what do I owe the honor, Mrs. Callahan?" Scott stood, rubbing his palms down the front of his jeans. "Or should I call you sis?"

Julia rolled her eyes. "You know who I'm talking about. She's fragile right now."

"You don't give her enough credit."

"She gives you too much."

Scott's jaw tightened because Julia was right. Even though Lexi had avoided him the past week, he'd seen her watching him when she thought he wasn't looking. Sometimes she'd catch him watching her. Either way, instead of the wariness she should have for him, her gaze showed nothing but trust. That was dangerous for both of them. He wasn't someone she could trust, and he didn't trust himself around her. Which made working and living with her a form of torture. But he couldn't walk away.

Not willing to admit any of this to Julia, he shrugged. "In case it matters, your little ray of sunshine propositioned me. I said no."

Julia's eyes narrowed. "Bull."

"It's true, ask her. Despite the fact that you and my big brother think I'm the bad seed of the Callahan clan, I don't want trouble in Brevia."

"You're nothing but trouble."

"From what I understand, you were a bit of the same back in the day."

"I've grown up."

"Who says I can't?"

She studied him, literally looked him up and down. After a moment, she said, "Stay away from her."

"I have every intention of staying away."

"You moved into my apartment."

"You and I are family. I have more right to it."

"I sublet it to her."

"That's right, you rented an apartment and gave a fresh start to the woman who tried to take your son away."

"I'm giving her a second chance."

"Maybe I'd like one, too."

"You betrayed Sam," she said after a minute. "In the worst way possible. He doesn't trust you."

Scott nodded. "I know that. What I did was wrong and I can't apologize any more than I have. That woman was bad news. The way I went about proving it to him was a mistake. But I don't regret breaking them up. She would have hurt him more than I ever did."

Julia's delicate features went soft. "He's a good man."

"And I'm happy he's found you. I'm glad you have each other."

"You were mad he didn't take the job with the Marshals because he wanted to stay in Brevia."

Scott nodded. "I was frustrated. I thought working with him would give us a chance to put the past behind us. But after meeting you and Charlie, I understand why he made the choice he did. I'm not mad anymore." Scott sighed. "I'd still like things to be better."

"He told me you're hosting a reception for us."

"He said you'd be against it."

"I'm not. I hated this town for a long time, but I'm

happy here now. Why not celebrate that?" She offered a small smile. "Will you come to dinner this weekend? I'll invite my mom and Joe, too. Vera is thrilled about the party. We can make plans then."

"Sure," Scott said, returning her smile. "I'm not so bad once you get to know me, Julia."

"Maybe," she answered, eyes skimming the bar. "This place looks a lot better."

He followed her gaze to the newly polished floor and the fresh coat of paint on the main wall. He'd put in a lot of hours this week fixing things up where he could. He liked the hard work and couldn't help but feel proud of how much he'd accomplished. "Thanks. We're going to start serving food in a few days. Open for lunch, too."

She nodded. "Anything that brings more people into downtown is good as far as I'm concerned." With a last look around, she turned for the door. "I'll see you later, Scott."

"A pleasure talking to you, sis."

She laughed and walked out into the late-morning sunlight.

Scott glanced at his watch. It was close to noon, which meant he didn't actually have to be here for nearly five more hours. Suddenly, another day of being cooped up in the bar was too much for him.

He poked his head into the back hallway. "Jon?" he called out.

"Yeah, boss." Jon came from the kitchen, wiping his hands on a towel.

"Do you think you can take care of things here for a few hours?"

A smile broke across the man's ruddy face. "I'd be happy to. I used to watch over the place for my dad."

Scott nodded and grabbed his jacket from a hook on the wall. "I'll be back before we open."

Chapter Seven

Lexi tossed the book she was reading onto the coffee table. Freddy yawned and stretched next to her. She had a whole day in front of her before she needed to get to work, but couldn't muster the energy to make decent plans.

She heard keys in the apartment's door and turned as Scott walked in. She'd thought he'd already gone to the bar for the day or else she would have been holed up in her room.

"Let's go," he said, pointing a finger at her.

"Go where?" She reached again for her discarded book, ignoring the fact that her heart had picked up its pace. "I'm kind of busy."

He gave her a lopsided smile. "Liar. Come on. We're going to have some fun."

"Can you clarify how you define *fun?*"

"Nope." He leaned over the couch and took her hand to gently pull her to her feet. Freddy stood up, tail wagging. "We'll see you later, buddy."

"Do I need to change clothes?" Lexi asked, smoothing her hands across her T-shirt and jeans. "It would help if I knew what to prepare for."

"We're going on an adventure," Scott replied, his eyes traveling up and down her body like a caress. "You look perfect."

Lexi's mouth went dry but she forced herself to smile. "Somehow that doesn't reassure me."

The truth was she was excited to go with him, wherever they ended up. She knew Scott was bad for her, or at least that was what he kept saying. But she trusted him to keep her safe no matter what. Lexi had never felt that with anyone in her life. It was an oddly freeing sensation.

"Grab a jacket and gym shoes. We don't want to be late."

After gathering her things, Lexi followed him out to his truck and climbed in, both excited and a little bit scared. She wondered if Little Red Riding Hood had felt the same way when she'd gone through the woods to Grandma's house. Scott drove through town and turned onto the highway heading into the mountains.

As the truck climbed the curvy road, Lexi gazed out the window to the forest below. Brevia sat in a valley nestled at the base of the Smoky Mountains. Although mornings were crisp this time of year, by noon the sun was bright in the sky, bathing the tips of trees in a golden light that made the whole area look more alive. She'd grown up in the city, gone to college there, too, so she found herself transfixed by the beauty of nature surrounding them.

Scott didn't say much as they drove, but the silence was companionable. Lexi was used to silence. Other than discussing current cases or other legal matters, her father didn't talk much to her. She often lived in her head and now found her mind wandering along paths of memories that were better left untraveled. Her father's harsh criticism and her fear that she'd never have the courage to truly live life out from under his thumb.

"Don't go there."

She jumped as Scott drew his fingers across her hand where it rested on the seat between them.

"Whatever you're thinking about, let it go today. We're going to have fun, leave the problems for later."

"It's hard not to think about things," she admitted.

"Have you gone on your date yet?"

She was taken aback by his question. "I can't talk about that with you."

"One of the other waitresses mentioned that Mr. High School Science Teacher is considered quite the catch."

Lexi shrugged. "We're supposed to go to a movie next weekend."

"You don't sound too excited."

She glanced at him from under her lashes, but his eyes were fixed on the road. "I'm very excited."

"Do you have a long list of qualifications for a potential suitor?" he asked, and she heard the smile in his voice.

"Actually, being with someone my dad didn't pick out for me is my top priority." She sighed. "My last…current…whatever boyfriend is a fourth-year at the firm. He wants to make partner in the worst way."

"He thinks making it with the boss's daughter will help his chances?"

"I can't imagine another reason he'd be so serious with me."

"Then he's an idiot." Scott said the words with such conviction that a little ball of emotion began to unwind inside Lexi's chest.

"Do you have a girlfriend?"

"Nope. I don't do relationships." He glanced over at her and winked. "I'm a bad bet, remember?"

"What about your brother's fiancée?" Lexi asked and saw his fingers tense around the steering wheel. "Did you fall in love with her?"

"I fell into bed with her," Scott answered candidly. "Not the same thing."

"Oh."

"I don't believe in love, Lexi. I'm not made that way."

She shook her head. "Everyone is made for love."

"For an attorney, you're kind of an idealist."

"It's not an ideal. It's true. There's somebody for everyone."

"Whatever you say." Scott pulled into a long gravel driveway and slowed to avoid divots on the well-worn track. A sign that read Smoky Mountain Adventures greeted them from the side of the property. They pulled up to a small cabin with several picnic tables in front.

"What are we doing?" she asked again, eyeing the row of shiny Jeeps and ATVs sitting next to an oversize garage. A corral of horses was situated on the side of a long barn, with a few parents and children milling about outside.

"We're going zip-lining."

Lexi clenched the door handle. "You're kidding, right?"

"Have you ever been?" Scott pulled into a parking

spot and turned the key, looking at her as the truck went quiet.

"I'm afraid of heights," she whispered.

He squeezed shut his eyes. "I didn't know that."

"If you'd told me our destination back at the apartment, I could have filled you in."

"That's okay," he said after a moment. "Even better, actually." He opened the driver's side door and hopped out.

Lexi would have followed him, but she was paralyzed in her seat. Her stomach churned as a bead of sweat made a slow trail down her back. She concentrated on moving air in and out of her lungs at a normal rate. She might have understated her fear of heights. Petrified was more like it. She could barely walk up an open-air flight of steps.

The door to her side of the truck opened and Scott leaned in. "Ready?"

"No."

"You can do this."

"I'm going to puke," she said, her voice a croak.

He smiled and raised his mirrored sunglasses onto the top of his head. His blue eyes looked into hers, total confidence in her radiating from their depths.

"You left your job, your home and moved to a tiny town hundreds of miles away where the only person you knew was a woman who hated you. You found a job, albeit one you're no good at and totally overqualified for, but it's a job. And for reasons unknown to me, everyone you meet loves you. Customers, the other staff, even the guy who delivers the beer asks about you."

"He does?" Lexi shifted in her seat. "That's so sweet."

"Sweet as pie." Scott reached across her waist and

unbuckled the seat belt. "If you can manage all of that in a couple of weeks, sliding down a cable is going to be a cinch."

Lexi dug her fingernails into the seat. "No way."

Scott's fingers found hers, easing them from their death grip on the leather. "You can do this. It's part of the adventure. Once-in-a-lifetime, bucket-list adventure. That's what you want, right?"

"I can't," she whispered miserably.

"Yes, you can." He dropped a soft-as-a-feather kiss on her mouth. "I believe in you, Lexi Preston."

She breathed him in, the crisp, male scent and the taste of mint on his lips. "I believe in you, too, Scott."

He tensed for a moment, then eased back. "Prove it. Let's take our mutual-admiration society to the zip line. I'll make sure you're safe the whole time."

She met his gaze and saw both a challenge and promise there. Sometimes she felt as if she'd spent most of her years avoiding the parts of life that scared her the most, whether it was something physical such as her fear of heights or, more terrifying, feelings and worries. Suddenly, this step represented so much more, and she needed to take it. She wanted to prove that she was worthy of his faith in her.

"Okay," she answered, her voice shaky with nerves.

She let him lead her to the front office, her knees stiff with fear as her insides churned. Scott filled out the paperwork and spoke to the tour operator, a tall man in his early forties with sandy-blond hair and a full beard. Lexi paced back and forth, reviewing legal briefs in her head to stop the panic from consuming her. She could overcome this. Look at how much she'd done in the past few weeks. This was just one more part of her adventure.

"Zach's going to take us out personally," Scott told her as the man disappeared into a room off the side of the main waiting area. "He's the owner, so it will be fine."

Lexi bit down on her lip.

"You can do this," Scott said again and wrapped one arm around her, his fingers tracing circles on her biceps.

"I thought you didn't want to hang out with me," Lexi said softly, grasping on to anything that would distract her from the thought of careening through the forest tied to a metal cable. "Why the change of heart?"

"I never said I didn't want to hang out with you," Scott corrected. "I said having an affair with me was a bad idea."

She looked up at him, searching his pale blue eyes. "So you want to be friends?"

"I don't really have friends, Lexi." He shrugged but kept his eyes on her. "I'm probably as bad at friendship as I am at dating."

"I don't have many friends, either. It would be new territory for both of us." She couldn't help the smile that curved her lips. "I think I'd be pretty good at it, though."

He studied her for several moments. Once again, everything else disappeared as she lost herself in him. "I bet you will." Taking a breath, he added, "We're friends."

Lexi's stomach tightened as she swayed the tiniest bit closer to him. She felt more than friendship for Scott, but she'd been honest about not having many friends. Hearing him say they were seemed like a good step. "You know, friends don't try to kill each other by making them do a zip line."

He took her hand in his and led her toward the front door. "I'm broadening your horizons," he said as they walked outside into the warming air.

Zach, the owner, was waiting in a four-person open-top Jeep. "Y'all ready?" he asked as they came down the steps.

"Sure are," Scott answered.

At the same time Lexi whispered, "Heck, no."

She climbed into the backseat and they headed up a dirt road behind the property. Lexi didn't realize how much Scott's touch had bolstered her confidence until it was gone. She wrapped her arms tight around her middle, trying to quell the panic that rose to the surface once more. Scott looked back several times and gave her a smile or wink. She wanted to climb up between the seats and bury herself in his lap.

After a few minutes, she began to see a web of cables attached to what looked like oversize telephone poles between the trees.

"Scott tells me you're nervous," Zach called back. "We're going to start with one of the shorter lines so you get used to the feeling."

Lexi nodded, but her fingernails dug into her back. When he said *going to start,* she got the distinct impression he expected her to do this more than once. She wondered briefly what would happen if she passed out or literally threw up. There were countless ways she could embarrass herself today, and she figured she had a good chance of hitting them all.

In another moment the Jeep stopped and Zach jumped out and began gathering harnesses and other equipment from the cargo hold. Scott offered her a hand to help her out of the backseat. She snatched hers back when he commented on how cold it was.

"It's going to be fine," he said softly, taking her hand again and warming it between his.

She was a ninny, no doubt about it. She bet the women he knew from his time in the military and the Marshals did stuff that would make this look like a walk in the park. She wanted him to know she was up for the challenge, even one that was so small in the grand scheme of things.

"Let's do this," she said and charged after Zach.

Scott couldn't quite believe the woman careening down the cable, whooping with joy, was the same person he'd practically had to drag out of the car a few hours earlier.

Lexi came to a stop on the landing of the last line and pumped one fist in the air. "That was awesome," she yelled and threw her arms around Zach. "Thank you so much for this," she said, hugging him hard.

As Zach's big hands moved a wee bit lower than was appropriate, Scott cleared his throat. "It was my idea, if you remember."

She turned to look at him, her smile widening. "Did you see me? I was flying. It felt like I was literally flying."

She came toward him and he grinned, thinking of her launching herself into his arms the same way. Instead, she punched him lightly on the shoulder, then danced in front of him, just out of reach. "I was so scared at the edge of the first zip line, but it was such a rush. That was the best day. Ever."

Scott's best day would actually include her pressed up against him, preferably naked. He inwardly shook his head. "I'm glad you liked it," he told her. "But we should head back."

They gathered the gear and walked toward the Jeep,

Lexi and Zach taking the lead as the older man regaled her with stories of other adventures he'd had.

"Maybe I'll try skydiving next," Lexi said with a laugh.

Scott wondered if somehow he'd created an adrenaline junkie, and it made him crazy to think that Zach or any other guy would be with her on subsequent escapades.

His eyes dropped to Lexi's jeans, specifically her hips swaying as she walked. He was a fool, he realized, to think that he could be her friend without his desire for her getting in the way. The more he told himself she wasn't his type, the more drawn to her he became.

He'd wanted to get away from town today, to forget everything from his conversation with Julia to the bar to his family and their expectations of him. The only person he wanted to spend time with was Lexi. She'd been avoiding him and he knew he should have left it at that.

Seeing her face down her fear today and come out on the other side of it more confident and proud had made him want her all the more.

If he could, he'd like to bottle up the light that radiated from her and save it for his darkest moments, like a perfect Scotch he could savor at his own pace.

It had killed him to watch both Zach and the younger man who'd helped them gear up flirt with Lexi, all the while knowing he had no right to stop it. She'd offered herself to him with no strings attached and Scott had been a fool to turn her down. Now the young guide, Matt, jogged up to Lexi. He leaned down to whisper something in her ear. She glanced back at Scott, then shook her head. Matt handed her a small piece of paper, grinning like an idiot until Zach shooed him away.

He watched Lexi tuck the paper into the back pocket of her jeans, looking over her shoulder and giving Scott a thumbs-up before turning away again.

Scott gritted his teeth. This friendship was going to be the death of him.

Lexi knocked on the door of Frank Davis's law office for the third time. She knew someone was in there because she'd seen the blinds move after she'd first knocked.

Finally, the door opened, revealing the older attorney, his button-down shirt wrinkled and a spot of what looked like mustard staining his polka-dot tie. He'd lost weight since she'd last seen him, but not in a good way.

"Hi," she said, holding out her hand. "You may not remember me but—"

"I remember you. You're the little girl who made a fool out of me on the Julia Morgan case."

Lexi stepped forward to prevent him from shutting the door in her face. "I'm sorry about my actions around the custody suit, but I think we can both agree that things worked out for the best in the end."

"I had it under control," he muttered.

"Like you do Nancy Capshaw's divorce and Ida Garvey's latest estate plan? Her will hadn't been updated in almost ten years, Frank. She had no living trust, nothing to protect her family's inheritance of her more recent investments."

His round eyes widened even further. "Listen here, missy, don't you go trying to steal my clients. You have no right. I could report you to the bar association for that."

"I don't want to steal any clients," Lexi said. She

glanced over his shoulder. "Could I come in for a few moments?"

"I'm busy right now."

Lexi might not have been the most assertive person in the world, but she pretended she was working for her father once again. Her fear of failing in his eyes always made her more forceful when dealing with people who didn't want to talk to her. Fear was a powerful motivator.

"I'll be quick," she said and easily slipped past him. She looked toward the receptionist's desk in the small lobby, which looked as if it had been deserted for months. A sad houseplant sat on the windowsill behind the desk, leaves brown and shriveled. "Where's your secretary?"

Frank let the door shut and turned to her. "She quit a while back. I don't need her, anyway. Brevia doesn't generate a lot of law business, not like it used to."

"Really?" Lexi found that hard to believe. In the past two days, since her meeting with Ida Garvey, she'd had a half-dozen messages from locals wanting help on a variety of cases. "Is there another law office nearby?"

He scoffed. "Of course not. I've been the main attorney in these parts for over twenty years. I built my life in this town. I've worked on every major case this county has seen." His finger jabbed into the air as if underscoring his importance. He looked around the office and sighed. "It isn't like it used to be. A whippersnapper like you wouldn't understand."

She glanced toward the inner office and sucked in a breath at the stacks of manila files lining the walls. It appeared that Frank hadn't put anything away since his secretary had left. "I understand your clients need an attorney who can keep up with their cases." She stepped forward. "I could help if you want."

His lips pressed into a grim line and she continued quickly, "I don't mean take over. But I'm licensed to practice in North Carolina. I've got time during the day...before my shift starts."

As she said the words, she realized how much she still wanted to work as an attorney. Yes, the bar was a fun diversion, something totally different than what she'd been doing. She was proving that she could take care of herself, and facing some of the demons left over from her childhood and what had happened to her mother.

But despite choosing to become a lawyer to please her father, in her heart she loved working with people and having the opportunity to help fix their problems. She'd lost sight of that in Ohio, when most of her work had been fighting for people who didn't deserve her help. People unlike the ones she'd met here in Brevia.

She realized she felt at home here, and the feeling didn't scare her. Even if it was for only a short time, she wanted to make a difference, pay it forward in her own way. Maybe that would give her some confidence for believing she could do the same thing once she returned to her own life.

"What do you think, Frank?"

"Are you crazy?" He slammed a fist into the wall, making her jump. "I see what you're doing here! You think you're the first young lawyer to walk into this office and pretend you want to help me?"

"I'm sorry, it's just—"

"I don't need your help. You think anyone in this town would ever trust you, with your background?"

"But you do need assistance." She took a calming breath, trying not to let his words hurt her.

"So what if I've slowed down a bit? I can keep up. Maybe I like to play golf a little more than I used to. I get the work done. And I'm my own man. I built this practice from the ground up. I'm not someone's puppet. I never did my daddy's dirty work, digging out every tiny bit of nastiness about the people I was working against."

"I didn't—"

"You're not the only one who can look into someone's background, Ms. Preston."

Lexi swallowed. "I did things I'm not proud of. I'm trying to make a better life here. I'm trying to start over, to learn from my mistakes."

He walked to the door and held it open. "Then you'd better learn it someplace else. You're not welcome here."

She clenched her fists, both from frustration and embarrassment. Her intentions here had been so good.

"What am I supposed to do when someone comes to me for help? I won't turn them away."

"Run along home to daddy, Ms. Preston. You don't belong here."

"I… You… This isn't…" Frank did nothing but stare at her, arms crossed over his chest.

Blinking back tears, Lexi fled from the office back into the street. She felt as if she were a young girl again, wanting nothing more than her father's approval, but being continually denied no matter how hard she tried to please him. She knew her past wasn't perfect, but wondered if she'd ever get to a point of being able to outrun it.

* * *

"What do you think of sweet-potato fries verses regular ones to go with the burger selection?"

Scott finished his inventory of bottles and turned. "Whatever you want, Jon. It's your kitchen."

Jon grinned at him. "We'll be open for lunch on Monday."

"Great. The sign guy is coming tomorrow to change the wording on the marquee to Riley's Bar & Grill." Scott picked up the stack of mail from the bar and began to leaf through it. "We need the bump in revenue to off-set all the cash I'm..." His voice trailed off as his eyes settled on a small white envelope.

"You okay, boss?" Joe took a step closer.

"Yeah, sure. I'm just thinking of when the new bar-stools are going to be delivered."

He picked up the envelope, his fingers holding it so tight that one corner began to crumple. "Can you give a call to the food supplier and confirm we'll need the fresh ingredients Monday morning? I don't want anything to go wrong with the rollout."

Jon studied him, but didn't call Scott out on his quick mood change. "Got it. I better get to work." He turned and hustled toward the kitchen.

Scott walked around the bar and sat on one of the high stools. He didn't have to open the letter to know what it contained, but he did, anyway. The short memo indicated that he'd have an official review in D.C. at the end of the month. It was scheduled two days before the reception for Sam and their father. The timing couldn't have been any worse, but Scott knew if he didn't show for it that his career with the Marshals was over.

He wasn't sure what he wanted his future to be, but he

didn't want the decision to be made for him. At the same time, he wasn't ready to talk about what had happened.

As if on cue, the front door of the bar banged opened.

"This day stinks," Lexi announced as she stalked through. Scott could almost see the smoke rising from her ears. "I try to help someone and he wants nothing to do with me. Totally ungrateful for my offer. It's ridiculous."

Scott wasn't sure if she was talking to him or about someone else, but her words hit home. "Not everyone wants to be helped," he muttered.

"That doesn't make sense," she said, her big eyes narrowing as she met his gaze. She took in the letter in his hand and came forward. "What's the matter? What happened?"

It bothered him more than he was willing to admit that she could read him so easily. "Nothing happened for you to worry about." He folded the letter and tucked it into his shirt pocket. Scrubbing his hand across his face, he forced his mouth into a smile. "What's got your cute panties in such a bunch?"

"You have no idea if my panties are cute or not."

"We're roommates." He winked at her. "You left a basket of folded laundry in front of the TV last night. I especially like the little pink ones with bunches of cherries on them."

Her mouth dropped open. "You shouldn't look at my panties, folded or not."

He'd like to do a lot more than look. He'd like to peel them from her hips and…

"I know what you're thinking," she said, pointing a finger at him.

"Honey, if you knew what I was thinking, you'd run out that door right this minute."

He loved the hint of pink that flushed across her cheeks. "Don't distract me. What was that piece of paper you stuffed in your pocket?"

"You're the one who came in here all hot and bothered."

"I had an awful conversation with Frank Davis. He won't admit he can't keep up with his caseload or why. I offered to help and he was rude."

"Offered to help? You want to practice law in Brevia?"

"Not forever. But I can ease some of his backlog. People are already coming to me. It's strange that there are no other law firms in town. It's like he's hoarded all of the business for himself but can't manage it anymore." She shook her head. "You're getting me off track again. Why are you upset?"

"I'm not upset," Scott said, standing and turning back toward the bar.

She grabbed his arm and pulled him around to face her. "There's a muscle pulsing at the base of your jaw. You're mad as heck about something. Maybe I could help if you told me what it was."

"I doubt it." He glanced at his watch. "Besides, your shift doesn't start for another hour. You shouldn't be here."

"I'm too worked up to go home. I came in to start on the plans for the reception. I need to burn off some energy."

"I know how you can burn off some energy."

She looked straight into his eyes. "I've already asked you for an affair. You said no."

"What if I've changed my mind?" he said, reaching out and pulling her close.

"What's in the letter?"

As fast as he'd drawn her to him, he pushed her away at those words. He walked from the bar to his small office, wishing for a way to burn off some of his own energy. As sunshine-sweet as she appeared, he knew Lexi could be worse than a dog with a bone. She wouldn't give up until he told her something.

As he expected, she followed him back. "You can tell me," she said quietly. "It's okay to let me in."

She was wrong. Scott wouldn't let anyone in, not even Lexi. But he answered truthfully, "It's a summons for a review from the Marshals office in D.C."

"To review what?" She lifted one hip onto the corner of his desk, clearly making herself comfortable. "I thought you were on a leave of absence?"

"An administrative leave," he clarified. "My partner died during a botched arrest. He was one of my few real friends at the agency. We'd gone through the academy at the same time."

"I'm sorry, Scott."

He hated sympathy. "It was my fault. Derek Sanchez was a good officer, a family man with a pretty wife and two small children waiting for him at home. The pressure of the job was bad enough, but trying to balance a normal life would take its toll on anyone."

"What happened?"

"He put himself in the line of fire instead of waiting for backup. It was stupid, a rookie mistake. He knew better but…"

"But?"

"Derek had been drinking the night before. We'd been

on a stakeout for days. Sitting around with nothing to do but think can drive you nuts, even in the field."

"He was drinking on the job."

"Technically, we had the night off. But it made him careless the next day."

"How is that your fault?"

Scott shook his head, stopped in front of her. Suddenly, he needed to tell someone…to tell Lexi…the whole story. "I should have stopped him, but he'd been griping for weeks about how his wife was busting his chops, pressuring him to take a desk job with the agency. I knew he needed to blow off some steam, so I didn't stop him."

"He was a grown man," she said softly. "You weren't his babysitter."

"I should have been his friend. I knew Derek had been drinking more than usual in the months before he died, but I wasn't much of a role model. I was trying to protect him, but as usual my methods left a lot to be desired. I fell asleep and left him alone. He drank a lot more than I'd realized. When things went down the next morning, he was in no condition to handle it."

"You think he was still drunk?"

"I sure as hell hope not, but I don't know. I never said anything. If it came out that he was at fault, it could've messed up his life insurance and pension. His wife… she needs that money."

Realization dawned in Lexi's eyes. "So you walked away from your career rather than expose his issues."

"It doesn't matter," Scott said, shaking his head. He balled his fists at his sides, the familiar frustration returning. "I let him down. Like I let everyone down."

She straightened, and Scott expected her to reach for

him, felt his whole body stiffen as he both feared and longed for her touch and the way it made him feel. She walked past him instead. He glanced over his shoulder, unable to help himself watch her walk away. Just like his mother had done to a seven-year-old boy who'd needed her more than she could handle.

Chapter Eight

But Lexi didn't leave. Her hand reached out and turned the lock on his office door. She returned to him and took his clenched hand in hers, trailing her fingers across his palm the same way he'd done to hers when she'd been frightened of zip-lining. His awareness of her almost overwhelmed him.

"Have you changed your mind, Scott?" she asked softly, her eyes still on their intertwined fingers.

He shook his head, forcing himself to ignore his need for her. "I'm not going to tell them anything about Derek. Even if it means I'll never work for the agency again."

She looked up at him now and her eyes held none of the judgment he expected to see there. "I meant about my offer."

He sucked in a breath and jerked back his hand, but she held tight.

"Do you," she asked, lifting his arm to place a whisper-light kiss on the inside of his wrist, "want to be with me?"

He nearly groaned. "It's not about what I want," he said with a ragged breath. "It's about what's good for you. I'm trying to protect you, Lexi."

"I don't need you to protect me." She stepped closer, taking his other hand in hers, then running her fingers up his arms until they curved around his neck. "I want you, Scott."

He knew he should walk away, but for the life of him, he couldn't move a muscle. "Don't do this," he whispered.

"What?" Her smile belied the innocence in her voice. She reached up and pressed her mouth to his. "Do you mean this?" Her body leaned against his as her scent wound through his mind, filling his head with the most amazing pictures of her moving underneath him. "Or this?" Her tongue traced the seam of his lips like an invitation.

He knew it was wrong, but he couldn't take any more of her sweet torture.

His arms tightened around her and he slanted his mouth over hers, taking control of the kiss. He felt her smile against him and melt into him even more, her desire stoking his until it was difficult to tell where he stopped and she began.

"Don't say I didn't warn you." He ground out the words before lifting her into his arms and carrying her to the couch pushed up against the far wall.

"This is all my fault," she agreed, tugging at the hem of his shirt even as he lay her against the cushions.

He stripped off the shirt and almost smiled at the way her eyes widened. "Having second thoughts?" he asked, sitting up a bit. If she was smart enough to stop this beautiful madness, he had no choice but to let her.

To his surprise, she leaned forward and lifted her own shirt over her head. "Not a single one," she said, watching him from eyes full of need and wonder. "I just hope I don't disappoint you."

Desire unfurled low in his stomach at the sight of her creamy skin under a peach-colored lace bra. "Seriously, how does a woman who dresses like a nun half the time have such great lingerie under her clothes?"

She rewarded him with a saucy smile. "It's my little secret and there's no one to tell me that I can't."

"If anyone tells you to stop, send them to me and I'll break all of their fingers." Scott placed his hand on her neck, feeling her pulse race. "You are so damn beautiful," he whispered.

"You don't have to say that." Some of the light in her eyes dimmed. "I know it isn't true."

When she would have turned her head, he cupped her face between his hands. "Lexi Preston, you are beautiful, desirable, smart and too kind for your own good."

Lexi wanted to believe him. Looking into his eyes, she almost could believe him. The desire she saw there made her bold. With trembling fingers, she eased her bra straps along her arms. Scott sucked in a breath as he reached behind her to unhook the clasp. The small bit of fabric dropped to the floor, suddenly making her self-conscious again. She covered her breasts with her hands until he gently pushed them away.

"I want to look at you," he whispered, his voice filled with something that sounded like reverence.

Lexi groaned softly as his hand covered one sensitive tip, rolling it between his fingers. "So beautiful," he repeated softly and lifted his head to flick his tongue across her heated skin.

She sucked in a breath and at that moment his mouth found hers, melding to her, and he pressed her bare skin along the length of him. He touched her everywhere, running his hands down her back, flipping her over and, in the process, easing her jeans and underpants down her hips. His clever fingers slid up her thigh and she gasped for air, his mouth over hers taking in her tiny moans as he touched her in ways she hadn't imagined.

He continued to kiss her as his fingers stroked her to a frenzy she couldn't control. All her inhibitions seemed to melt away until there was nothing left but sensation and feeling, her entire body throbbing with need.

"Let me hear you," he said against her mouth, speeding the rhythm of his fingers against her.

As if at his command, her body arched and bright pleasure tore through her, shattering her senses. He held her close as her arms and legs trembled, finally coming back to herself and settling under him once more.

He kissed her softly, nuzzling her neck with his mouth and whispering gentling words to her. "You are amazing."

"We didn't…" she began, embarrassed at her body's intense reaction to him. "You didn't…"

"Not here," he told her, raising himself onto his arms above her. "You deserve more than a roll on my office couch."

She looked toward the ceiling and mumbled, "I like your office couch."

He laughed, dropping a kiss on her forehead. "Then you'll love my bed."

She glanced at him then. "So this isn't over?"

He straightened, his eyes heating once more as his gaze traveled across her body. "We haven't even gotten started."

A knock at the door had Lexi jumping, grabbing for her clothes.

Oh...no.

She was naked in her boss's office. How much more clichéd could she be? "This is bad. What was I thinking?"

Scott picked up her shirt and handed it to her. "You weren't thinking. Neither of us were." He pulled her to him, kissing her once more. "We're going to do more not thinking together later." Then he unlocked the door, slipping out before whoever was on the other side could see that he wasn't alone.

Lexi took a steadying breath as she pulled on her jeans, then smoothed her hair back into a ponytail. She felt terrified and elated at the same time. Good-girl Lexi Preston having a go at it on the job. She put a hand over her mouth to suppress a nervous giggle. Finally, it felt as if her adventure was really beginning.

Lexi took another order from a table of regulars. They were a group of guys from a local construction company who came in for a weekly boys' night out. She liked the harmless flirting, and when one of them grabbed her hand and loudly kissed it, she laughed before drawing back.

She'd been in Brevia for two weeks and still reveled in how invigorating her new freedom made her feel. A few nights earlier she'd indulged in a dinner of chips, soda and cookie-dough ice cream, savoring the choice to do something her father wouldn't approve of, even it was a tiny stake in the ground of her independence.

She'd been embarrassed when Scott had walked in midfeast, then surprised when he'd grabbed a spoon from the kitchen and helped her polish off the pint while watching some cheesy reality TV show on cable. He hadn't tried to kiss her or made any kind of move, but hanging out with him had been so easy and right that her heart had opened to him even more.

But she'd been avoiding Scott since the encounter in his office, too afraid of her own feelings to pursue anything more with him. Realizing she needed to keep better control on her emotions, she turned away now to collect the table's drink orders, but Misty hauled her off to a corner of the bar.

"What's going on with you and Scott?" the other waitress asked on a hiss of breath.

"I… We… Nothing," Lexi answered quickly. "Why?"

"He just about came over the bar when that guy grabbed you." Misty shook her head. "He looks like he wants to throw you over his shoulder and carry you off."

"A little too caveman for my taste." Lexi laughed as her pulse started to race.

"I wouldn't mind being carried off by that man," Misty said with a knowing smile.

Lexi's gaze tracked to the bar. Scott handed two beers to a couple sitting at the stools in front of him before his eyes met hers. One side of his mouth curved up and the promise in his gaze made Lexi's knees go a tiny bit weak.

"That look isn't nothing," Misty said, whistling softly under her breath. She chucked Lexi on the shoulder. "I don't know how you did it, girl. Most of the waitresses and half of the female customers have been angling for a way to catch Scott Callahan since he got to town."

"And you think I've caught him?"

Misty smiled. "I think you're darn close." She winked at her. "I just hope you know what to do with him once you've got him."

Lexi swallowed hard as Misty walked away. She had no idea what to do with Scott. The things her imagination conjured made her tingle from her toes to the top of her head.

She waited until he was busy at the other end of the bar to retrieve the drinks for a table up front. She'd gotten them balanced on her tray when a familiar voice spoke behind her.

"I can't believe I raised a common barmaid."

She managed to hold the tray steady as she turned to face her father. "What are you doing here, Daddy?" She glanced behind him to see Trevor Montgomery, her onetime boyfriend, standing in the wings. "And you've brought reinforcements. How lovely. Grab a table and I'll get your order after I deliver these drinks."

Her father reached for her. "You'll speak to me now, Lexi, and not to take my order. You're coming home."

"I'm working right now," she said, her spine stiffening. "We're busy tonight and I can't keep the customers waiting." She held her tray in front of her, pushing past her father and Trevor. She brought the drinks to the table, then motioned to Misty. "Could you cover my section for a few minutes?"

Misty looked to where Robert Preston was glowering next to the bar. "Sure thing, sweetheart."

Lexi made her way back to her father, dread making her legs feel as if they were encased in cement. Lord, how she wanted to just run out the front door. She knew her father was serious about her coming home, but she'd never thought he'd actually show up in Brevia to collect her. She'd been stupid and naive to think he'd actually respect her decision. Respect for her wasn't part of Robert Preston's makeup.

"I have return tickets on the late flight out of Charlotte," he told her when she stood in front of him. "We're leaving now."

"You just got here," she answered weakly, pretending not to understand

He shook his head. "Let's go, Lexi. Trevor will drive us to Charlotte, then return to Columbus with your car. You're lucky he's willing to take you back after the way you deserted him. You're lucky we both are."

Trevor's eyes darted to her father before returning to her face. "I've missed you, Lex." He gave her a placating smile.

"Give me a break, Trevor. I doubt you noticed I was gone, besides the fact that you had to find a new way to brownnose my father." She shook her head. "Dad, I'm not going back yet. I told you that on the phone. I want a few more weeks."

"That's ridiculous."

"You're the one who sent me away."

"You ruined the relationship with one of our best clients." He looked around with clear disdain. "What is it about this town that attracts you?"

Lexi forced her gaze to remain on her father. Out of the corner of her eye she could see Scott with a group of men at the far end of the bar. "People are nice here. It feels real. I feel real."

"Nonsense," her father scoffed. "Your life is in Ohio

with me. The firm needs you. I didn't pull you out of the gutter only to have you return there."

"This isn't the gutter, Dad, and you didn't pull me out of anywhere."

"Your birth mother was a common bar whore, Lexi. A stereotype of the worst sort. I saw something more in you." He paused, his eyes narrowing. "The adoption agency thought I'd be happier with a boy, but I chose you. I invested in you. Don't make me regret my decision."

"I'm not a piece of property." Her voice caught and she swallowed, trying to get ahold of her emotions. Robert Preston could smell weakness in an adversary and would gladly use it to his advantage. She knew that better than anyone. "I'm your daughter."

"Which is why I can't understand how you could disobey me in this way."

"I'm not trying to disobey you," she argued. "I just need time."

"Time is up and you're coming with me."

She shook her head and backed away. "No."

He reached for her arm, but someone stepped between them.

"She said no." With Scott looming in front of him, her father took a step back, his eyes wide with disbelief.

"This is none of your business," her father said on an angry breath.

"Anything that happens in my bar is my business."

"It's okay, Scott."

He glanced at her. "Are you sure?"

She nodded, wiping at her eyes.

Scott turned to Lexi, his thumb smoothing a tear off her cheek. "You're safe here, you know."

"Safe?" her dad sputtered. "I'm her father, you idiot. I'm the one who keeps her safe."

"I'll take care of this," Scott told her. "You can go in back and get yourself together."

She nodded. "I'll let you know my decision about my future in a few weeks, Dad. Don't contact me again before that."

"Come back with me now or I'll make sure you have no future. Not in the legal community, anyway." He pointed at Trevor. "Do something, you oaf. Ask her to marry you."

Trevor looked visibly shocked, but stepped forward. "Lexi, would you…?"

Her head started to pound. She knew Trevor was her father's henchman, but hadn't realized how far his loyalty went. "You don't have to do that, Trevor. I'm not going to marry you. Now or ever."

He sighed, probably with relief. "I'm sorry, Lexi," he whispered, and it might have been the first honest thing he'd said to her the whole time they'd been dating.

She turned away, expecting her father to follow, but found herself alone, leaning on the hallway wall outside the kitchen. She stifled a sob, then jumped when Jon popped his head out of the kitchen. "You look like hell."

"I feel worse," she answered.

He shifted uncomfortably, then offered, "I made an apple pie earlier."

She smiled, grateful for the simple gesture. "A slice of pie is just what I need."

Scott turned to Robert Preston. "Leave her alone."

Preston's eyes narrowed. "I know you, Callahan, and you aren't the Boy Scout your brother turned out to be."

"This isn't about you or me. It's about Lexi."

"I think you're part of the reason she doesn't want to come home."

"I don't give a damn what you think."

"You should." Preston smiled, but it was a mean look on him. "I have contacts in D.C., you know. Some with the U.S. Marshals agency."

Scott felt a muscle clench in his jaw. "So what?"

"I know why you're hiding out here. Based on your history, I'd guess running a bar in Brevia, North Carolina, isn't going to cut it for you. You need action. I can help you."

"You don't know anything about me."

"I know you have a snowball's chance of getting back to active duty without a recommendation from the review board." Preston's smile widened as Scott flinched. "I want my daughter back. I didn't realize how serious she was until tonight. I'm not used to seeing Lexi with a backbone."

"It looks good on her."

"In your opinion. But she belongs with me. Her life is in Ohio, not down here." Preston sighed. "I'll give her the month she wants. I'm not stupid. But at the end of the next few weeks I want her to return home. I want you to make sure she does."

"She can make her own decisions," Scott answered, tension balling low in his gut. This guy was a real piece of work. No wonder Lexi needed to take such drastic measures to gain some sense of independence.

Preston nodded in agreement and reached in his wallet to hand Scott a card. "Let's make sure it's the right one. Call me when you come to your senses."

Scott pocketed the business card. He didn't plan to do

anything with it, but Preston didn't need to know that. Right now, he just wanted him out of his bar. "If you knew me at all, you'd know I can't be bought."

Robert Preston only smiled, then turned and walked out of Riley's Bar. Scott hoped it was the last time he'd ever lay eyes on the man.

He looked around the crowded room, surveying the changes he'd made, as well as the groups of people laughing and mingling throughout. In truth, he hadn't missed the action of the field as much as he thought he would. Renovating the bar had taken his time and energy and given him an outlet that was more satisfying than he'd thought it could be. He liked belonging somewhere, getting to know the regulars and making this place part of the community.

The menu was already a success, with local business people coming for lunch and families in the early evening. He'd talked to a couple of local bands and musicians about hosting an open-mic night, and he'd put some events on the calendar to draw people in during the week. Carving out a place in Brevia was good, but he also wondered how long his desire to stay would last. Scott had a long track record of leaving people and places behind. After things were stable, would Brevia still hold his interest? Preston was right that this wasn't the life he'd imagined for himself.

Lexi took another bite of the apple pie, then washed it down with a long drink of milk. "This is fantastic," she told Jon from her seat at the large work island in the middle of the kitchen. "You're a genius."

"Don't plump up his ego too much," Scott said from the doorway. "I've already given him one raise."

Her eyes darted to Scott. "Is my father...?"

"He left, Lexi."

Both disappointment and relief rolled through her. "I guess that's good."

"He's giving you the time you want. He's going to leave you alone for a month."

She nodded. "But he's not interested in me until I come back to Ohio."

Scott didn't answer and his silence told her everything. She took another bite of pie, swallowing back her emotions.

"It's his loss," Scott said quietly.

"Thank you," she answered. She pushed away the half-empty plate and stood. "I need to get back out there. Misty can't cover everyone."

"It's thinned out. People are going home early. She'll be fine."

Lexi took her plate to the sink, then turned to give Jon a small hug. "Thanks for the pie and the company. Your food is going to make this place a huge success. I bet your dad is smiling down on you right now."

A broad grin stretched across the older man's face. "I'm glad you think so. You're a good person, Lexi. I hope your father comes to his senses."

She tried to smile, then swiped at her eyes. "I need to pull it together," she said with a shaky laugh.

Scott took her hand as she came into the hall, tugging her toward the back exit. "Where are we going?"

"Home," he answered, pulling harder when she would have stopped.

"You have a bar to tend and I can't just leave because my dad's a jerk," Lexi argued. "I'm going to pull up my big-girl panties and—"

"Max will finish up the night behind the bar," Scott told her as he opened the door to the alley. "He'll appreciate the extra tips. Misty and Tina can cover the floor. You've had the rug yanked from under you and my day wasn't much better. We're taking the night off. I'm picking up carryout and you can choose the movie."

She dug in her heels as the door shut behind her. Scott turned.

"You don't have to do this."

She squared her shoulders as he studied her. She tried to look brave and tough and unbreakable. All the things she didn't feel.

"I want to," he answered softly. "I want to be with you, Lexi. God help us both, because I know I should leave you alone. I knew it that first night I banged on the apartment door. I can't offer you much, but you deserve your adventure or whatever you call it. Especially if you're going back to make nice with that nasty old coot you call a father. I'm going to make sure you have some fun before that happens."

She hated that her lip trembled at his words, that what he said touched some deep, hollow place inside her. It didn't matter that Scott couldn't offer her much, because living with her father had made her believe she wasn't worth anything. She tried to lighten the mood by asking, "How about a Hugh Jackman movie?"

"As long as he's not singing."

"Let's go for the first *X-Men,* then. It's my favorite."

"You like superheroes?" Scott looked doubtful.

"Only on the big screen," she promised.

He drew her closer, but instead of kissing her he wrapped his arms around her and buried his face in her hair.

"I'm sorry your father is a schmuck."

She laughed despite the emotion welling in her chest. "That about sums it up. But I stood up to him. That's something, right? I'm still here whether or not he wants me to be."

"You are," Scott agreed. "Now let's get that food."

Hours later, Lexi glanced up into Scott's sleeping face. His long lashes rested on the smooth skin of his cheek, while a shadow of stubble covered his jaw, making his perfect features more human. With his eyes closed, his face had a sense of vulnerability he made sure to keep hidden most of the time. He was strong and tough and so alone.

She understood that last part. Despite all her plans and pledges about a big adventure, she was scared to death to be by herself. She didn't know who she was and she wondered if she'd like the person she'd find at the end of her journey.

She was tucked in the crook of his arm, where she'd been through most of the movie. They'd shared Chinese takeout and a couple beers before settling in to watch Professor Xavier and his crew save the world.

If Scott's intention had been to give her some distance from the pain of her father's rejection, it worked. She still felt the hurt, but it wasn't so raw. It was like a prism she could hold out in front of her and study, see the sharp edges and places where feeling unlovable had torn at her soul. But now she could place it on the shelf, add it to her collection of emotional scars.

Maybe that was what someone who'd been physically abandoned by one parent and emotionally rejected by the other did. Lexi was a pro at compartmentalizing her feelings, on tamping them down until she could be in control enough to do what everyone around her expected.

Scott was different. He bulldozed through his emotions, trying to run fast enough that they couldn't touch him with their demanding tendrils. The two of them were so different and yet alike in many ways. That could explain the connection she felt for him. She didn't have to polish herself to a glossy shine for Scott. He'd take her as she was, broken parts and all.

That final thought gave her the courage to lean up and trace his face with her fingers, then press her mouth to his. After a moment he stirred, moaning softly.

She lost her nerve at the sound of his voice. This was stupid. Women like her weren't meant for seduction. But when she would have scrambled away, his arms came around her, grabbing her tight to him and pulling her across his lap. His hands wound through her hair, his mouth devouring hers. She couldn't get enough of him and she pressed herself along the length of his body, straddling him so she could feel his desire for her. She needed him so badly. He made her feel whole and right. She wanted to capture that feeling and carry it with her all her life.

He gripped her face until she looked into his eyes. "I want you, Lexi. I want this. Now."

"Now," she agreed with a soft intake of breath.

He lifted her easily and she clung to him, ripping at his shirt as he made his way down the hall to her bedroom. He tore away the quilt and lowered her gently onto the bed. She lifted her blouse over her head, then watched as he stripped away his shirt. His jeans and boxers followed a minute later. She felt her mouth drop open at the sight of him. Muscles bunched and rippled across his chest, and her eyes caught on the tattoo banding one firm biceps. His whole body was strong, hard and ready. The breath whooshed out of her lungs as desire pooled low in her belly.

She'd had a couple boyfriends over the years, but nothing had prepared her for the sight of Scott Callahan.

A hint of a smile played around his mouth as he watched her watching him. "You can't leave me standing here all alone like this. Aren't you going to join me?"

She reached for the waistband of her pants, then stilled. "I don't know... I'm not you—"

"Thank the Lord for small favors," he said with a laugh and came toward her. The look in his eyes could only be described as predatory.

Slowly, he moved his hands up her legs to the top of her cotton pants, then bent forward to kiss the tip of one nipple through the lace fabric of her bra as he slid her slacks down her legs. He leaned back as he reached her knees. "Each part of you is perfect," he whispered. "And I plan to become intimately familiar with every inch."

"I hope you're not disappointed," she said, then shut her eyes, embarrassed that he might think she was fishing for a compliment.

"Nothing you do could disappoint me, Lexi. I want to touch you. All of you. But only if you're sure." He bent toward her once more, his kiss soft and exploratory, as if giving her time to change her mind.

"Open your eyes," he said against her mouth.

He sat back and she couldn't help reaching out to run her palm across his taut stomach muscles and up the hard planes of his chest. She could feel his heartbeat, strong and steady under her hand. A small grin curved her lips as she watched his blue eyes darken with desire the longer she touched him.

He swallowed and let out a ragged breath that was almost a groan as she grazed her fingernails along his skin. He was giving her time, she knew, to get her bearings…to take control of this moment between them. His ability to understand her needs, even at a time like this, melted her heart. The knowledge that he wanted her as much as she did him gave her the courage she needed to pull him to her again.

But when the tip of her tongue touched his and her legs wrapped around his body, his mouth turned hot and demanding.

She put out her hand to pull the sheet over them, but Scott ripped it away. "We don't need that."

He trailed his mouth down her neck, along her collarbone and over the swell of her breast. At the same time his hand traced a path up her thigh until his fingers found her core. He teased her until she almost lost control.

"Wait," he whispered into her ear. "Not yet."

He grabbed his jeans from beside the bed and pulled out a condom, ripping it open with his teeth. A moment later he balanced above her once more, and his mouth captured hers at the same time as he entered her. She couldn't tell if the groan of pleasure came from her lips or his.

As if their bodies were made for each other, they moved together. A sensation built low in her stomach as the rhythm intensified. For the moment, they were one, and she reveled in the feel of his body over hers, the sparks of pleasure firing through every part of her. After several minutes, she couldn't hold back any longer and her release echoed through her, followed by Scott's harsh intake of breath. He whispered her name and then his head fell to the pillow next to her, nuzzling against her ear as he said words of endearment.

She'd never known anything like what she and Scott had just experienced together. She knew now what true freedom meant. And that no matter what her future held, she'd hold this night close to her heart for the rest of her life.

Chapter Nine

Lexi was able to keep her feelings about her father at bay for the next week. Her feelings for Scott were another story. Things seemed to speed up, both at the bar and between them. They worked to finish renovations, then spent every night together.

As much as she loved being in Scott's arms, her favorite times were the morning. They'd take turns making breakfast, then walk Freddy through the park, talking about everything and nothing. Scott told her about his mother's death, his stint in the army and the work he'd done for the Marshals Service. His life had been an adventure already. He'd seen so much of the world and had to take care of himself in a way she couldn't imagine. Her life up until now had been so structured.

But he seemed just as fascinated with her life as she was with his. She realized, for all the moving around and excitement, what Scott lacked was a sense of being grounded. She thought maybe the bar did that for him, gave him a sense of purpose. She hoped their time together gave him a sense of home. But if she delved too far into sticky emotions, she could feel him pull away. It didn't matter, she told herself. Her time was ticking, anyway, and she'd have to make a decision about her life.

It was becoming clear that going back to the way things had been wasn't enough for her anymore. She didn't want to give up her law career, but working for her father would suck her down the same black hole she'd finally clawed her way out of. She put together a résumé and began to send it out, using contacts she had from the law community and law school. She applied for positions both in big cities and smaller towns, although nothing in her hometown of Columbus, Ohio. She was too afraid of her father finding out and sabotaging her plans. Several of the openings were in D.C. And Charlotte. She knew it was stupid, but hoped that being in one of those cities might enable her to continue to see Scott after her time in Brevia was done.

She also continued to advise locals, despite Frank Davis's not wanting her to. She couldn't turn away people who needed her help, and she was learning which aspects of the law were most appealing to her. She liked the variety that being a general counsel in a small town afforded her, liked using her skills to help people with their problems.

Scott told her she was being taken advantage of again, since all the work she'd done so far was pro bono. But she didn't care. It was important for her to believe she was making a difference.

She'd just finished up a meeting with Ida Garvey in

one of the back booths at the bar when the front door opened and Julia, her mother and her sister, Lainey, walked in.

It was late afternoon, so other than Lexi, Ida and Scott, the place was almost empty. The reception to celebrate the two weddings was only a couple weeks away, so Lexi expected they'd come in to discuss that. She sank down in her chair a little. Scott had asked her to help with the plans for the reception from a logistical end, and she'd actually enjoyed discussing everything with Julia. But she'd managed not to be around when Vera had come by previously. While Lexi had made amends with Julia, she had a pretty good idea how the rest of the family felt about her, and it sure wasn't friendly.

"Don't let Vera scare you," Ida said with a knowing smile. "She's mostly bluster."

Lexi looked at her client. She'd come to enjoy her weekly meeting with the older woman. Sometimes they discussed her estate, but often Ida filled her in on local gossip. She knew everything that was going on in Brevia. Julia had warned her that Ida was a busybody, but Lexi liked hearing her stories.

She watched Scott greet the three women, then his gaze met hers and he motioned her over.

She groaned softly. "I've got to be a part of this. It was good to see you, Mrs. Garvey. I'll get those motions filed, but you should really talk to Frank. I know he doesn't want me working with his clients."

"He'll deal with it," Ida said with a scoff. "He's gotten plenty of my business and more of my money. If his practice was so important, he'd spend more time on it."

"He's a good attorney," Lexi offered. "I still think you should talk to him."

"Too nice for your own good," Ida mumbled. "Go see to those Morgan women, dear."

Lexi stood and walked toward them. Vera was talking to Scott, pointing to something in a file she'd laid across the bar. Julia smiled, but her sister, Lainey Daniels, narrowed her eyes as Lexi came closer. She'd met Lainey only once, when she and her husband, Ethan, had come in for dinner. Lexi had seen some promotional photos Lainey had taken of the bar for a marketing campaign focusing on the tourist season in Brevia.

"Everything looks good for the reception," Lexi said to Julia. "I confirmed the time with the band yesterday and asked Scott to order the champagne you wanted for the toast."

"Thanks, Lexi." Julia smiled again and turned to her sister. "She's making me look totally on top of things with Mom."

"I still don't understand why she's in charge," Lainey answered, keeping her eyes trained on Lexi. "We all want to trust her but are you sure about this?"

"It's different now." Julia gave Lainey a pointed look. "You should know people can change."

"I agree with your sister," Vera interjected, taking a sip from the glass of water Scott had placed on the bar. "Julia, you've always been too trusting of people. It's gotten you into trouble in the past."

Lexi shook her head. "I'm not here to cause trouble, Mrs. Callahan. I want everything to be perfect for your celebration."

"Besides," Julia added, "I trust her a lot more than I do Scott."

"He's making changes to this place that are going to help the local economy for years to come." Lexi looked at Julia. "You know bringing more people into downtown is good for all the businesses here, including your salon."

"He's a loose cannon." Julia crossed her arms over her chest. "I don't trust him."

Scott cleared his throat. "I'm standing right here."

"I see you," she said. The look she threw him made Lexi smile. "I'm hoping you'll leave."

He tossed down the towel he'd been holding. "Gladly." His gaze met Lexi's, warming her from her toes up. *Good luck,* he mouthed to her before disappearing into the back.

"If you do anything to hurt my daughter, you'll have to answer to me," Vera said, turning her full attention on Lexi.

Before she could sputter out an answer, Ida Garvey's shrill voice rang out. "Vera Morgan, give the girl a break. It wasn't too long ago that your daughters were practically duking it out in the middle of town. Everyone deserves a second chance."

"Since when did you become anyone's champion, Ida?" Vera asked.

Lexi felt like repeating Scott's comment that she was standing right in front of them. But Julia caught her gaze and shook her head slightly.

"She's been helping me with changes I'm making to my estate plan. You know Frank Davis hasn't been up to snuff for a while now. That's what makes me her champion," the older woman said with a smirk. "I'm in it for what's best for me."

"Same old Ida," Vera muttered.

"But she's working for you, too," Ida retorted. "You'd see that if you weren't so hardheaded. She's got a whole file with the details of your reception. She's put a lot of thought into it. Half the town is going to be here to celebrate with you. Lexi's the one making sure it will be a night everyone will remember. Give her a chance, Vera."

With a small pat on Lainey's back, Ida shuffled out the front door. Lexi wasn't sure why it meant so much to her to have a woman she'd known for only a few weeks come to her defense, but it did.

Vera's gaze moved to Lexi. "Is this true?"

She nodded. "Yes, ma'am. I hope so."

Julia's mother motioned her forward. "Let's see what you've got then."

Lexi opened up the file where she kept her plans for the Callahan and Callahan reception. She'd never put together a party of this size before, but the organizing and details appealed to her analytical side. Plus, the busier she kept, the less time she had to spend worrying about her future. So when Scott had asked her to handle the celebration, she'd jumped at the chance.

As she pulled out her notes, her excitement overtook her nervousness regarding Vera's reaction. Most of what she was showing her Julia had already approved, so Lexi felt a bit more confident. "Julia told me your favorite color is yellow and hers is blue, so that's what I went for with the color scheme." She took out samples of fabric from the tablecloths and napkins. "Obviously, we're in a bar, and the whole event is a casual, homey family affair, but I still wanted it to be elegant." She glanced at Vera from under her lashes. "Because you seem like a very elegant lady."

"Agreed," she answered.

Julia and Lainey both laughed.

"There will be fresh flowers and candles at every

table—understated, but they should look beautiful in the light. I contacted the microbrewery over in Asheville, and they're supplying beer for us. They've agreed to brew a special Amazing Animal Ale for the event and donate a portion of their profits back to your shelter."

Vera nodded. "I like it."

"Congratulations on your wedding, by the way. Joe seems very nice."

"That's why I married him."

"It means a lot to Scott to be here with his dad and Sam." She looked at Julia. "They're all hanging out, you know."

"I know."

"Joe loves his boys," Vera stated. "He'll do anything to make up for how things used to be. He wants it to be right between them."

"Scott wants that, too. He's worked hard on the reception. I think he sees it as a way to prove to both of them that he's changed."

The older woman studied her. "You seem to know Scott pretty well."

"I work with him almost every day," Lexi said quickly, hoping nothing on her face gave away her true emotions.

"And they're roommates," Julia said.

Lexi saw Lainey choke back a laugh. "You're sharing the apartment with Scott?"

"It's not like…"

"Like what, Lexi?" Julia leaned forward and whispered, "Are you sleeping with him?"

Lexi tried to no avail to stop a blush from creeping up her cheeks.

Lainey shushed Julia, then put a hand on Lexi's shoulder. "Julia doesn't have good personal boundaries."

"And you're one to talk, little sister."

"You've obviously put a lot of work into the reception," Lainey continued, ignoring Julia. "I appreciate your help." She glanced at their mother. "We all do. Right, Mom?"

Lexi blinked back tears as Vera smiled.

"Julia's right that we believe in second chances. We also take care of our own around here. You're included in that now. Scott's family, too. If the two of you make each other happy, we're happy for you."

"I'm not staying in Brevia." Lexi choked on the words, but knew she owed these women the truth. "Scott knows that. What we have...whatever it is, it's temporary."

"You aren't staying?" Lainey looked confused. "But you fit."

"I don't know where I fit. That's what I'm trying to figure out."

Lainey gave her a quick hug. "I know how that feels, so I hope you do." She turned to her mother. "Come on, Mom. I want to show you the dress I picked out for the reception."

"Thank you for everything you've done." Vera pushed away Lexi's outstretched hand and gave her a hug.

"Oh." Lexi breathed out the one syllable, overwhelmed with emotion that these women could forgive her so easily for what she'd put Julia through. That they could accept her with her faults and all.

When Vera and Lainey walked out, Julia turned to her. "That wasn't so hard, was it?"

Lexi swallowed. "You're lucky to have the family you do."

"It took me a while to realize it." She nodded. "But you're right. Speaking of families, have you spoken to dear ole dad lately?"

"He was here a few nights ago. He ordered me to come home with him."

"And yet you're still here." Julia chucked her on the shoulder. "You have more backbone than I gave you credit for."

"You and me both," Lexi agreed. "I'm coming into the salon to see Nancy before my shift starts, by the way."

"She's grateful for all you've done to help with her divorce."

Lexi shrugged. "It wasn't that much. But she offered to give me a complimentary cut and color as a thank-you."

"Hallelujah!" Julia reached out and tugged on Lexi's ponytail. "It's about time you stopped wearing it pulled back."

"It's professional," Lexi argued.

"It's boring." Julia's eyebrows wiggled. "I bet Scott likes it down."

"He says... Never mind." Lexi blushed under the other woman's scrutiny. "I'm a total fool, starting something with him. I know it already so you don't need to tell me."

"You know as well as anyone that I've had my share of romantic missteps. Big ones." Julia glanced toward the back of the bar. "I know Scott has had problems in the past, but maybe he'll surprise us all. Either way, you're a big girl. You get to make your own mistakes."

Lexi nodded. "But it wasn't a mistake coming to

Brevia. Thank you, Julia, for giving me a do-over. No matter what happens, I'll always be grateful."

"No mushy stuff. Just buy me a drink if I ever get a night out on the town again." She shrugged at Lexi's questioning look. "My mom and Lainey help with Charlie during the week, but I haven't found an evening sitter he likes."

"What about me?"

"What about you?"

"I could watch him. I'm off tomorrow night. I can come over or you can bring him by the apartment."

"I wouldn't want—"

"Please, Julia. It's the least I can do. I swear you can trust me with him. You and Sam can have a date night."

Julia took a deep breath as Lexi found herself holding hers. Suddenly it was very important to her that Julia trust her enough to babysit Charlie.

"That would be great," Julia said finally. "I'll see if Sam can get off, and text you about the time."

"Perfect." Lexi glanced at her watch. "I need to get to my appointment. Are you walking back to the salon?"

Julia nodded. "Let's hit it."

"I need to…" Her eyes strayed to the back of the bar.

"Oh." Julia rolled her eyes. "Give lover boy a kiss goodbye for me."

"It isn't like that."

"I'm kidding, Lexi." She smiled broadly, then laughed. "Sort of. Either way, I'll wait for you outside."

Lexi walked to Scott's office, but stopped just outside the doorway. Suddenly she felt nervous, wondering if Scott would even care that she was going. Sure, they'd spent every night together for the past week, but it wasn't as if they were dating. More like roommates with benefits, which she supposed should make her feel cheap. But it didn't.

She peeked her head in as Scott looked up from the paperwork on his desk. "Hey there, gorgeous."

Lexi glanced behind her to see if Julia had followed her down the hall.

"I'm talking to you, Lexi." Scott came around the desk and toward her, as if he meant to replay their previous interlude on his couch.

Her breath caught in her chest and she held up her hands, palms out. "I have a hair appointment," she said quickly. "I just wanted to say, um…goodbye, and…"

Her mind went blank for a moment as he reached out and drew her to him, his mouth claiming hers in a deep kiss. After a moment he asked, "How did it go with Vera and Lainey?"

It took a few seconds before Lexi could even remember who Vera and Lainey were. "They're happy with the plans, I think."

Scott cupped her face with his hands. "That's because you've done an amazing job of organizing everything."

"Vera doesn't seem to hate me anymore."

"If she's happy, my father will be over the moon."

"Would you believe Ida Garvey came to my defense?"

"You have the ability to wrap just about anyone around your little finger," Scott said, kissing her again.

"Are you wrapped around my finger?"

"What's it look like?"

She thought about that for a moment. "Like I'm a convenient place to land at night."

He stilled. "You think I'm with you because you're convenient?"

"It's easy for both of us, right?" She didn't like the

sparks shooting from his blue eyes. "It's not as if we're dating."

His eyes narrowed. "So it's just sex for you?" His tone was incredulous.

"I didn't say that. But we haven't exactly been out to dinner or a movie or the stuff people do when they're dating. I'm not complaining. We're friends." She smiled to try to lighten the mood. "Like you said, the kind with great benefits."

"Friends," he repeated ominously.

"I need to go," she said, backing out of his arms. "We can talk about this later. Or not."

"Tomorrow night." He crossed his arms over his chest. "You're off. I'll get someone to fill in for me. We're going out."

"I'm busy tomorrow night." She bit down on her lower lip. "And that wasn't a very nice way to ask me on a date."

He shook his head. "Busy with what? And if you say a date with the high-school teacher, we're going to have a problem."

A little butterfly danced through Lexi's belly. "I canceled my date with Mark. I... It wasn't the right time for me." Was it possible that Scott Callahan was jealous over her? The mere thought made her want to giggle. "I'm babysitting. For Julia and Sam."

"Whoa. Didn't see that coming." Scott looked absolutely stunned and Lexi couldn't blame him.

"I owe Julia a lot." She paused, then added, "And I like kids. You've met Charlie. He's adorable."

Scott nodded. "Another time, then."

She nodded, but wondered if she'd freaked him out so much that there wouldn't be another time. The thought made her heart sink a bit, but she forced a smile. "I'll see you later, then."

He nodded and she turned to go.

"Lexi?"

She glanced over her shoulder.

"Don't do anything crazy with your hair," he said softly. "I like it just the way it is."

More butterflies took flight and she hurried out the door.

Scott knocked on the door to his brother's house, then wiped his damp palms across the front of his jeans. This was ridiculous. He'd seen combat zones, drug takedowns and everything in between. This night was nothing in comparison.

So why was his heart beating like crazy?

Before he could come up with a reasonable excuse, the door opened to reveal his brother in a pale blue button-down, striped tie and khaki pants.

"A tie?" Scott asked, whistling softly. "That's laying it on a little thick, don't you think?"

Sam huffed out a breath, then pulled at the collar of his shirt. "It's called making an effort, numskull. You should try it sometime."

Scott laughed. "Too bad I won the genetic lottery in our family. With a face like mine, showing up is all the effort I need."

"Is that so?" Sam looked unimpressed. "Then tell me why you're here tonight."

"I thought Lexi could use some help." He kicked his toe at an imaginary rock. "She practically begged me to come with her."

"There are different kinds of effort, Scott." Sam tugged at his collar again. "But I'm glad you're here."

"Because you still don't trust her?" Scott's fists clenched at his sides. "That's not fair if you—"

"Simmer down, bro. I trust her well enough. Lexi Preston is suddenly Julia's new best friend, and from what I've seen, she's making up for lost time, being helpful and kind and all that stuff." Sam stepped back and motioned Scott through the door. "I'm glad you're here because it's about time my son got to know his uncle. Julia's brother-in-law, Ethan, has quite a head start, so you've got some work to do."

Scott felt his nerves sound off like soldiers in a battle line. "I don't do kids, Sam."

"You're here."

"Obviously my first mistake." He shook his head. "Don't get me wrong. I'm happy for you. I'm sure you're a great dad. You were always so damn responsible and honorable and, well, everything I'm not. I think you'd be smart to stick with Ethan to play the doting uncle."

"We'll see. Charlie's pretty irresistible."

"I'm immune to cute." At Sam's raised eyebrows, Scott amended, "Kid cute, that is."

"Lexi's not your usual type."

"She's not."

As if sensing his sudden urge to bolt, Sam backed off. "I like her, Scott. You're obviously happy with her and you deserve some happiness."

"I don't want—"

"You can deny it all you want, but it's written all over your face. It's not a bad thing to care about someone. It took me a long time to realize that. Dad, too. We Callahans are kind of stupid in the face of scary things like love and emotions. But it's not so bad once you get the hang of it."

Scott couldn't help but laugh. "You missed your calling as a poet."

"You'll see," Sam said, giving him a light punch on the shoulder. "Come on in. They're back in the kitchen. Julia and I have a reservation awaiting us."

Scott followed Sam through the Craftsman-style house, wondering if he could be happy with a regular life. He hadn't been there since he'd first come to Brevia. Most of the time he'd spent with Sam or their father had been at the bar, either having lunch or watching a game. He couldn't believe how domestic Sam had become, his home filled with overstuffed furniture and framed photos on the bookshelves. It made Scott's body ache in a way he didn't understand.

This was never what he'd wanted for himself. He liked the thrill of the chase, the adrenaline high he got from putting himself in danger through his work. He would have never guessed that Sam could make a life for himself in a town like Brevia, and he certainly didn't understand the longing he couldn't seem to shake.

That need intensified as he walked into the kitchen to see Lexi seated in front of a high chair, talking softly to Charlie as the boy ate small mouthfuls of macaroni and cheese. She looked so beautiful with the early-evening light reflecting off her strawberry-blond hair. She looked as if she belonged there.

He wanted to belong, too.

"Daddy," Charlie yelled when he noticed Sam. "I got macan for dinner."

"Looks good, buddy." Sam walked over and bent to kiss the top of Charlie's head, a gesture so natural it made Scott's throat burn. "Miss Lexi is going to have help with you tonight. Buddy, do you remember meeting your uncle Scott?"

Charlie gave Scott a toothy smile, then held up a spoonful of macaroni noodles.

Lexi turned, the blush that was now so familiar to Scott creeping up her neck. "What are you doing here?"

"Reinforcements," he answered simply.

"Sam, we need to go if we're going to…" Julia came in through the back door, but stopped when she saw Scott. "Well, well. What have we here?"

"Be nice, Juls," Sam said quietly.

"One of the bartenders wanted to pick up an extra shift so I…I'm here." Scott crossed his arms over his chest, hating the feeling of being the center of attention in this cozy scene. "If it's a problem I can leave."

Julia flashed a knowing smile. "I don't have a problem. Lexi, do you have a problem?"

Lexi shook her head, but kept her attention focused on Charlie.

"Then let's go, hot husband of mine." Julia crooked a finger in Sam's direction. "I have plans for you." She bent forward and kissed Charlie's cheek. "Be good for Lexi, my little peanut. Mama loves you."

"Bye, bye, Mama. Loves you," Charlie answered and offered her a spoonful of macaroni.

"I love you, too, sweet boy." She looked at Lexi. "We won't be late. Bedtime at seven with a bath first and—"

Sam wrapped one arm around her waist and steered her toward the door again. "You've left a detailed list. They've got our numbers. It's all good."

"Have fun, you three," he called over his shoulder as the door shut behind them.

Charlie raised himself in his high chair to watch them walk out. "All gone," he announced and went back to scooping up his dinner. "Charlie thirsty."

Lexi straightened. "How about some milk, sweetie?"

The boy nodded.

Scott stepped forward, needing to be occupied with something. "I'll get it. Is there a bottle or…?"

"He's almost two," Lexi said with a small laugh. "There's no bottle." She went to the cabinet and pulled out a plastic cup with a lid. "He uses a sippy cup. They don't spill."

"I have some customers who could benefit from one of those."

Lexi filled the cup with milk, tightened the lid and gave it to Charlie. Then she turned to Scott. "I'm going to run the bath. Bring him upstairs when he's finished with dinner."

Scott grabbed her arm as she went to move past. "You're not leaving me here with him. Alone."

She smiled sweetly. "Reinforcements, remember?"

The way she studied him, Scott knew she was well aware of how uncomfortable he was. What had he been thinking? It was true that one of his bartenders, Max, wanted to make extra money. But there was plenty at the bar to keep Scott busy even when he wasn't serving drinks. Not to mention that several single women came on a regular basis and made no secret of flirting with him. If he'd wanted to occupy himself, there were better ways than babysitting for his brother. In truth, what he wanted more than anything was to be near Lexi. He'd do just about anything to have more time with her.

He had no intention of letting on, though. "Sure. Right. We'll be up in a bit."

With a small shake of her head, she left him alone in the kitchen with Charlie. His nephew. Scott sat on the edge of one of the chairs and watched the toddler as he would have a key witness, not wanting anything to go wrong when he was in charge.

"Relax," Lexi whispered as she peeked into the room once more. "He's a little boy, Scott. He won't bite."

"He might."

"Just have fun with him."

She disappeared again and Scott thought about all the ways he'd had fun in his life. Babysitting had never once been on that list.

Julia's dog, Casper, came to sit next to him, his gray snout almost level with the high-chair tray.

"Good doggie," Charlie said and threw a piece of macaroni in the air. Casper promptly jumped up and caught it, his stubby tail wagging. Charlie exploded into a fit of giggles.

"Um…" Scott said slowly. "I don't think you're supposed to feed the dog your dinner."

Charlie laughed again and threw another noodle, which the dog caught. More laughter erupted and Scott found himself smiling.

He picked up a noodle off the tray. "I once knew a dog who could do a special trick, Charlie. Let's see if Casper knows this one.

"Casper, stay," he commanded, then carefully placed the noodle on the tip of the dog's snout. "Wait," he said slowly, then gave the "Okay" command. Casper flipped the noodle off his nose and caught it.

Charlie squealed with delight. "Again, Unc-le. Do it again."

Scott's heart clenched the tiniest bit at the word *uncle*.

As much as he didn't want them to, that word and the boy who spoke it meant something to him. Reconnecting with his dad and Sam meant something. Something more than simply proving he wasn't the schmuck they both assumed him to be. Scott wanted to make it right with his family. He wanted to be the man no one believed he could become.

No one except Lexi. Since that first night in the bar, she'd seen more in him than he'd seen in himself. It made his gut clench to think he had only a couple more weeks with her. For just a moment he entertained the idea that it didn't have to end. What would it be like to make it really work with Lexi? Could he give that much of himself?

He didn't know for sure, but right now he wanted nothing more than the chance to try.

He did the treat-on-nose trick with Casper until there were no more noodles left on the tray.

"Up," Charlie said, raising his arms above his head.

Scott took a breath. Okay, he could do this. He carefully placed his hands under Charlie's arms and lifted, then cradled the small boy against his chest. Charlie immediately wiggled to be let down, and when Scott put him on the floor, he headed for the stairs.

"Baaf-time," the toddler announced as Scott followed on his heels.

"Would you grab a couple of towels from the hall closet?" Lexi called as they got to the second floor.

He did, then made it to the bathroom as she lowered Charlie into the tub. "Have you ever done this before?"

"No," she answered, her eyes never leaving the boy. "But I think I can manage." She handed Charlie an assortment of rubber toys and squeezed excess water out of a duck-shaped sponge.

Scott leaned against the counter and watched Lexi in action. She and Charlie sang several verses of "The Wheels on the Bus" as the little boy sat in the tub.

It was strangely intimate in a heart-tugging way to be a part of such an everyday routine in his nephew's life. Scott thought Lexi had never looked so beautiful. Her hair was pulled back in a loose ponytail, with several tendrils escaping to curl around her face. It was lighter since she'd been at the salon today, highlighting her pale green eyes even more. She laughed as Charlie splashed, leaving the front of her pink T-shirt sprayed with water.

"You'll be a great mother one day," Scott said softly, not realizing he'd said the words out loud until she turned to gape at him.

"I hope so," she said after a moment, her eyes so full of tenderness he wished he could stop time so that she'd always look at him that way.

Still, it scared him. Lexi made him want things he never expected to have and couldn't believe he deserved. He'd always managed to ruin the relationships that meant the most to him, so why did he expect anything would change now?

"I'm going to clean up the kitchen," he said and left the bathroom before she could see how much she meant to him. How much he longed for the stability and caring she represented. How he couldn't bear the thought that he was bound to ruin her, too.

Chapter Ten

Lexi finished putting Charlie's dump-truck pajamas on, pulling the bottoms over his diaper. She picked him up and snuggled her face into his neck for a few seconds, reveling in the scent of clean boy. Scott hadn't reappeared since he'd practically run from the bathroom earlier. She knew there wasn't much to clean up in the kitchen, so figured this whole night had freaked him out beyond the point of no return. She half expected that he'd left a note downstairs and already escaped to the bar, where he was much more comfortable.

She bit down hard on her lip to avoid tearing up again when she thought of Scott telling her she'd be a good mother. It surprised her how natural the role felt. She had so little memory of her own mom and found it hard to believe that she had any genetic instincts for parenting. But taking care of Charlie gave her an indescribable joy, while at the same time it left a deep ache in the core of her heart. It was one of many revelations from her time in Brevia. She now knew that, one way or another, becoming a mother someday topped her list of priorities.

She sat down in the rocking chair in the corner and read two books to Charlie, then turned down the lights and slowly swayed around the room with him in her arms, singing softly. When she felt his head grow heavy on her shoulder, she placed him in his toddler bed, dropping a soft kiss on his forehead before turning to go.

Scott stood in the doorway watching her, his eyes cast in shadow so she couldn't read them. He held out his hand and she laced her fingers through his, closing Charlie's door most of the way before following Scott down the stairs.

"I can't believe I'm saying this, but hanging with Charlie is almost fun." He led her to the living room and sat on the couch before pulling her down next to him. His arm wound around her shoulders and he dropped a kiss on her hair, a gesture so unconscious it made her feel they'd been a couple for years instead of weeks.

"He's amazing," Lexi agreed. "You must have quite a knack, too, because I could hear him laughing the whole time I was running the bathwater."

"Kid whisperer. Just one of my many talents."

She laughed and snuggled in closer. After a moment she asked, "Do you remember much about your mom?"

She felt Scott's breath hitch, but he didn't pull away. "I was so young when she died, there's not a lot of details. Mainly random snippets. I can recognize the perfume she wore, and she loved the Beatles, so certain music brings her back to me." He drew his fingers up and down Lexi's arm. "But I try not to remember that it was my fault she died."

Lexi tried to sit up so she could turn around and look at him, but he held her tight.

"My dad doesn't blame me. I think Sam used to. Either way, it's the truth."

"You were seven. She died in a car accident, right? How could it be your fault?"

"My dad worked all the time back then. His whole life was the force. It scared the hell out of my mom. I think she was afraid of being left with two boys to raise alone. She drank every night. My dad either ignored it or didn't want to admit there was a problem. But Sam and I knew, even as young as we were. I could see she wasn't right. Sam compensated by being the perfect kid. He tried to anticipate her every need, make life easier for her, to take away the stress."

"He was just a boy," Lexi said sadly.

"It was his nature." Scott gave a humorless laugh. "Not me. I was mad and I pushed all of her buttons. There was only room for one of us to get the attention from being a good kid, and Sam had that locked up. I went the opposite way. But I still didn't want her drinking. I don't remember my exact thinking, but I knew the bottle wasn't helping her cope with life. She'd hide the liquor and I'd find it and dump it. It would make her so angry, but I couldn't stop. I thought if the alcohol wasn't around then maybe she'd have a chance to get better."

"You were trying to help in your own way."

"The night she died she and my dad had a big fight. She went to get another drink, but I'd poured the rest of the bottle down the sink. That's part of why she drove off that night, to make a liquor-store run to replenish her stock. She wasn't far from the house when the accident happened. If she'd just been at home, she would have been safe."

He said the last words with a ragged intake of breath.

Lexi turned, looking into his eyes, so full of pain and guilt. "You were a kid," she said gently, wanting to reach out and touch him, but too afraid of breaking this moment and scaring him away. "You wanted her to get better."

He looked miserable as he said, "My good intentions didn't save her. If I'd just left her alone, maybe she would have stayed home that night. Maybe she'd never have died."

"It wasn't your fault," Lexi told him. "Children aren't responsible for the actions of their parents. Trust me, I know that better than anyone."

He lifted her hand off his cheek and placed a kiss on the inside of her wrist. "Do you remember your mom?"

"Only a little. An image here and there. But not much more than that. My father—big surprise—sent me to a psychologist when I was younger to 'process' what had happened to me. Basically, I was told not to dwell on the past and to be grateful for my new life and the second chance I'd been given." She sighed. "Which I was. I still am. But there are questions I wish I could have answered about her. I never knew my biological father and sometimes I wonder where I came from, who I'd be if Robert Preston hadn't molded me into his perfect, obedient daughter."

"You're more than the person he tried to make you." Scott said the words with such conviction, Lexi couldn't help but believe them. "You have a good heart and a kindness that has nothing to do with your father. You're stronger than he knows. If nothing else, you must have learned that since being here."

She swallowed around the lump in her throat. "I never thought of myself as anyone besides Robert Preston's daughter. But now I do. Holding Charlie tonight made me see that I have more to give than I could have imagined."

"But you still plan to go back to Ohio?" Scott asked, as though he'd read her mind.

She stood, the familiar feeling of nervousness coursing through her body. "It's like my time here hasn't been real. I've told myself it was just a break, something temporary, which made it not quite as scary. The thought of really being on my own, that's terrifying." She paced back and forth in front of the couch. "My dad is the only family I have. That's important to me. What would it be like if I had no one?"

"You have me," Scott said quietly.

She stopped and turned to him. "Do I really? What if I told you I was applying for jobs in Charlotte and D.C. so I could stay close to you? Would you stick around if you thought I wanted more than a couple of weeks of fun? You've made it clear you don't have anything more to give."

"You deserve something—someone—better." A muscle ticked in his jaw. "Of course I want time with you. But I've told you before, I mess things up for the people who care about me. Your life is just starting. I'm not going to ruin it for you."

"I don't believe that," she said, feeling her temper rise. "I think that's an easy out you've given yourself because you don't want to do the hard work a real relationship takes."

His eyes went dark. "I can't give you what you want. Isn't it enough—"

He stopped midsentence as the front door opened. Sam and Julia came into the living room, holding hands.

"We're back," Julia called out. She paused, her gaze traveling between Lexi and Scott. "Rough night?"

Lexi shook her head. "Charlie was wonderful. It all went great."

Sam watched the two of them, then threw a pained look at Julia. "She's totally lying."

"I'm not," Lexi protested. "Did you have a good dinner? You're back so early."

Now Sam's expression turned soft as he gazed at his wife. "Dinner was great, but…"

"We're so boring," Julia finished. "We just wanted to come home and watch a movie on the couch."

Scott stifled a yawn. "How old are you two, anyway?"

"That doesn't sound boring," Lexi argued. "It sounds perfect."

"Would you like to join us?" Sam asked after a moment.

Julia elbowed him in the ribs. "Ignore him. He's being polite." She turned and planted a deep, wet kiss on Sam's mouth.

"She's right," he agreed, his arms tightening around Julia. "You should go now."

"Um…right." Lexi grabbed her purse from the side table.

"Get a room," Scott muttered.

"We have a whole house," Julia countered. But she turned and placed a hand on Lexi's arm. "Thank you for watching Charlie tonight. We needed this."

"It was my pleasure," Lexi answered.

"If you stay in Brevia awhile, we'll try a long week-end." Sam laughed when Lexi's eyes widened and Scott groaned. "Think you can handle it?"

"Have a nice time, you two." Scott put his hand on the small of Lexi's back and guided her out onto the porch.

She kept walking down the steps and toward her car, suddenly feeling exhausted. She yearned for the kind of love Sam and Julia shared, but was afraid she'd already given her heart to a man who could never let himself feel the same thing back.

"Hold on," Scott said, tugging on her hand. "Don't leave mad, Lexi."

"I'm not angry." She pulled away and kept moving. "I'm tired. I'll see you back at the apartment."

"Is this our first fight? Should I sleep at the bar to-night?" His tone held a hint of teasing she couldn't return.

"I'm not sure what this is, Scott. I know what I want, but it's up to you to decide whether you can give it to me." She unlocked her car, then looked back at him. "When you figure it out, let me know."

She pulled up to the curb outside her apartment building. Scott had disappeared shortly after they'd left Sam and Julia's street. She wondered if he really planned on sleeping at the bar. There were bound to be several women willing to let him warm their beds if he needed a place to stay. The thought filled her with a hollow feeling of disappointment.

He'd told her he was bound to disappoint her, so who was truly to blame?

She'd hoped for something more even though it was foolish. He hadn't made any promises, but he'd smiled when she told him she was applying for jobs in D.C., answering her unspoken question about their future with a kiss. The way he looked at her, the way he held her close every night made her believe they could have one. He might not say the words out loud, but she knew he cared for her.

Every morning for the past week he'd warmed her towel while she was in the shower, leaving it ready for her on the sink when she got out. It was a small gesture, but to her it represented the essence of Scott. He could be cool and detached on the outside, but he had the softest heart of anyone she'd ever met.

Now her own heart ached at the thought that she wanted things Scott would never be able to give her.

She sat in the car for several minutes before climbing the steps to her apartment. The wind blew cold as darkness fell. A light mist that promised more rain enveloped her, giving the air a heavy weight that matched the pressure in her heart.

This evening had started out with so much promise and now here she was, alone again. Just as she put the keys in the lock, a noise behind her made her turn. Scott stood at the end of the hallway, a bouquet of fresh flowers held out in front of his chest.

"I thought you'd gone to the bar," she whispered.

"I'm sorry," he said as he walked toward her. "I'm sorry I don't have all the answers, that I'm not a better man."

"I like you just the way you are." Her voice cracked as he handed the bouquet to her. She knew suddenly that she didn't just like him. She loved him. The vulnerability and need in his eyes called to a place inside her, and there was nothing she could do to resist the pull.

He scooped her into his arms and she clung to him as he carried her into the apartment, kicking the door shut. His mouth captured hers with a kiss so possessive, so commanding, it stole her breath. But she met his desire with all the emotions she'd banked up inside. Everything she wanted to tell him but was too afraid to say out loud she tried to show him through their embrace. He seemed to be filled with the same hunger she felt for him. The flowers dropped to the floor as they tore at each other's clothes and he carried her to her bedroom.

Her breasts tingled as he slid his hands over them, over her entire body, trailing kisses in the wake of his skilled fingers. When he moved over her, inside her, she knew that in embracing her freedom she'd also lost her heart to this man. Whether or not he could ever truly be hers didn't matter as they found a perfect rhythm, a connection she knew she'd only ever find in his arms.

He whispered endearments into her ear, coaxing her to the highest peaks of pleasure before finding his own release. He continued to kiss her, lightly and softly. He nuzzled her neck and threaded his fingers through her hair, pulling her close as he sank back against the pillows.

Her head lay on his chest and she could hear his heartbeat, as wild and erratic as she knew hers to be, until it finally settled to its normal pace. She wondered for a moment if anything would ever be normal inside her again.

She knew he wasn't sleeping because he continued to run his fingers lightly over her bare back.

She tipped up her head after a moment. "I've never had make-up sex before."

He grinned wryly. "So I guess now you're going to want to fight all the time."

"Only if you promise to bring me flowers and apologize so enthusiastically."

He shifted her onto her back once again. "Enthusiastic? You haven't seen anything yet."

And for hours more, he proved to be a man of his word.

Scott whistled as he loaded cases of beer into the big refrigerator off the kitchen. It was midmorning and the bar was quiet, his favorite time to get work done.

"Someone's in a great mood today."

He turned to Jon Riley with a grin. "It could be because I just ran the numbers for last month. We're doing better than I ever expected on revenue. I think that has a lot to do with your menu drawing in new customers. I appreciate everything you've done, Jon."

The older man shrugged, looking embarrassed to be singled out. "You've made some great changes here. My father would be happy to see his place thriving again." Jon made a show of checking supplies in the food pantry. "But I'd guess your attitude has more to do with a certain tiny redhead."

Scott went back to stacking boxes. "We're trying to keep it quiet, you know. She's only here temporarily, but I'm the boss and I don't want it to look…" No matter how he tried, he couldn't stop the smile that played across his lips. "Truth is, I don't care how it looks. She's amazing."

"Everyone can see that you two belong together."

"The hell they do."

Scott's back went stiff as he glanced to where Robert Preston stood in the doorway of the kitchen.

"I assume you're talking about my daughter," Preston said through clenched teeth, "and I'm here to tell you she belongs back home with a man who is worthy of her. Not with some washed-up ex-combat soldier stuck in this town."

"Your daughter gets to make her own decisions now," Scott argued. "You don't own her anymore. You never really did." He stepped toward the man. "You have no business here, Preston."

"I want to check on Lexi. Make sure she's doing okay. I assume she's ready to come back. If you've kept up your end of the bargain in making sure she knows what's best for her."

"She told you she'd make her decision at the end of the month. You agreed to leave her alone until then."

Preston glanced around the kitchen, derision clear in his gaze. "If her choice is the life she left behind or this, I know what she'll choose. I didn't raise her to settle for someone like you. I can offer her safety, security and a guarantee that she'll have a decent future."

Anger coursed through Scott. "Your problem is you underestimate her. Does the name Reid and Thompson mean anything to you?"

"It's a D.C. firm started by one of my old partners. So what?"

"What if I told you Lexi had an interview with them?" She had said she wanted to keep her interviews quiet until she got an offer, but Scott knew she'd get hired and couldn't help but gloat to her father. He enjoyed seeing Preston's face turn blotchy.

"You think you're her only option, but what you forget is Lexi is a hell of an attorney in her own right. There are plenty of places that would be glad to hire some-one with her talent. I'm not saying that I'm worthy of her. She's better than either one of us deserves. Maybe now that she's out from under your thumb she'll have enough confidence to believe in herself." He paused, then drove the final nail in the coffin. "Maybe you've already lost her."

Preston stalked toward him, looking as if he was ready for a fight. As much as he'd enjoy pummeling this man who'd caused Lexi so much pain, Scott wasn't that stupid.

"You think you know her so well." Preston spit the words, his face only inches from Scott's. "She needs me. I'm her only family and that means something to Lexi. She'll come to her senses one way or another." His mouth curved into a nasty grin. "And what about you? Hiding out here from your past. This isn't what you want. You need to be where the action is. Do you really think it's all going to work out so easily for you?"

"Maybe this is enough for me." Scott forced his voice to remain even. "You don't know who I am."

"We'll see about that." Preston turned and walked from the room.

Scott stood there, his fists clenched tightly. Robert Preston had hit the heart of Scott's biggest fear. That he was going to mess up this chance he'd gotten at a new life, that the broken part of him would bubble to the surface and cause him to destroy the connections he'd built. That was why he'd chosen to be a loner in life. It was easier to take care of only himself, leaving less chance of collateral damage for the people around him.

He may have been only a boy when his mother died, but he knew he was the one who'd driven her away, even as he'd wanted to save her. When he'd tried to show Sam that his fiancée was no good, Scott had ended up almost ruining his relationship with his brother. And he'd wanted to protect his partner to the point that he'd turned an unintentional blind eye to the drinking that had eventually killed Derek.

He'd opened up to Lexi, let her into his life and heart because he'd believed it was a temporary arrangement. But he knew she wanted more from him, and he desperately wished he could give it to her. She filled the dark corners of his body and soul with her light. She'd become a lifeline back to the world for him, away from the isolation he'd lived with for so long. What would he risk if he fell for her completely? There was a good chance he would eventually hurt her. Scott wasn't sure if he knew another way, despite his best intentions.

Even if he couldn't hold on to her, he knew for damn sure he wasn't going to let her father reclaim her.

"He's intense," Jon said, pulling Scott back to the present.

"He's like a poison to her," he answered. "Toxic."

"Lexi certainly seems happier and more confident than when she first arrived." Jon laughed softly. "She doesn't drop glasses anymore."

Scott felt a smile play at his lips as he thought back to her first bumbling shifts at the bar. "This isn't where she was meant to be, either. It's just a short-term stopping point on her journey."

"What if the path leads to her father again?" Jon asked.

"She can't go back there."

"Maybe you should give her a reason to stay."

Chapter Eleven

The bead of sweat that trickled between Lexi's shoulder blades had nothing to do with the sun beaming through the clouds. The weather was growing colder, but this morning felt almost perfect. Leaves shimmered on the trees in the park and Freddy played with a pinecone, batting it around with his nose as she sank onto the park bench.

She held her cell phone in her palm, still staring at it, unable to believe the conversation she'd just had. When the Human Resources department from one of the firms where she'd applied had called earlier this morning to tell her she hadn't gotten the position, Lexi had been surprised but not too disappointed. She had several leads on open positions at reputable law firms. But after that first call, her phone had rung almost on cue every fifteen minutes, with all the openings suddenly drying up or the positions going to other applicants.

The final call had come in from the senior partner at Reid and Thompson, her father's former colleague, who'd informed her that they had no room for her at their law firm. When she'd questioned him about the reason, his answer had been cryptic, but he'd eventually suggested her best option might be to head back to Ohio to try to patch things up with her father.

She dialed her dad's private line now, the sinking feeling in her chest expanding as he answered on the first ring.

"Are you ready to come home?" he asked, cutting right to the heart of the matter.

"How did you know I was applying for other jobs? Are you having me followed?" She bit her lip as emotion threatened to overtake her. She wouldn't give him the satisfaction of hearing how upset she was. "Why, Dad? Why sabotage my chance at a fresh start?"

"I want you here with me."

"I have to learn to live on my own."

"You're all I have, Lexi." She heard him draw in a breath, as if he was shocked he'd admitted that much to her.

"I'm your daughter and I love you," she whispered, willing him to accept her right to choose her own life. "Where I live won't change that."

"You don't belong there. Especially not with him."

"Are you talking about Scott?" She adjusted the phone in her hands, realizing her fingers were shaking. "Leave him out of this, Dad. He cares about me."

Her father barked out a bitter laugh. "Always so naive. That's part of the reason you still need me. The man you think cares about you is the one who told me about your job prospects."

Lexi shivered from the ice that suddenly ran down her spine. "When did you talk to Scott?"

"I paid another visit to Brevia and Riley's Bar. Your boss was very interested in how I could help him return to his real life as a marshal. I still have quite a few contacts in the Justice Department, you know."

"What did you do, Dad?"

"It's time to come home, Lexi. Your little adventure is officially over."

She hung up, stunned to think that Scott would have betrayed her this way. He'd been encouraging her to apply to law firms in the region, bolstering her confidence and making her feel as if she could really contribute if given a chance. He still wouldn't talk about a future with her, insisting she needed to worry about herself before she made any relationship a priority. But Lexi had continued to hold out hope that his feelings for her, or the ones she believed him to have, would be enough to make him realize their relationship was worth taking a chance on.

Now any future they could have had together was ruined, so much collateral damage—just like her heart. She knew he didn't love her; he couldn't with what he'd done. She also knew that as much as she loved him there wasn't a way to repair this kind of betrayal.

Still, she had to know why.

Her hands were shaking as she started walking, Freddy trotting along at her side. She didn't stop until she was in front of Riley's Bar & Grill. Part of her wanted to keep going, to return to the apartment and pack as much as she could fit in her suitcase. She wanted to escape this place and the sad, desperate promise she'd believed it held for her.

She couldn't outrun her past, couldn't pretend it wasn't waiting to swallow her again. She'd gotten what she came for—adventure and a taste of freedom. But now that was done and nothing could change the future she'd tried so hard to avoid.

Scott stood behind the bar, his full attention captured by whatever he was reading. He looked up as she walked through the door, tenderness shining in his eyes. Their light made her heart break even further, creating a wide chasm so painful she clutched a hand to her chest to tamp down some of the pain.

It didn't work. Nothing could lessen the hurt she felt. Nothing but the truth.

"You're not going to believe this," he said, coming around the bar. "The Marshals office has reinstated me. Apparently, their investigation has been satisfied without my review." He reached for her, but she stepped away. Freddy, traitorous canine, wiggled at Scott's feet.

"Was it worth it?" Her throat was so dry the words came out as croak.

"Hell, yes, it was worth it." His smile brightened and he crouched down to pet Freddy. "I didn't have to rat out my partner. I didn't ruin his family. I'm in the clear."

His words were another blow, so much like a punch to the gut that she bent forward with the force of it.

"Lexi, what is it? Come sit down."

"Don't touch me," she said with a painful hiss of breath when he tried to gather her close. "You ruined me. You destroyed us. And you're telling me it was worth it?" She shook her head. "You're no different than my father. I thought—"

"What are you talking about?"

How could he look at her as if he gave a damn? Her

pain turned to anger, which gave her the strength she needed to straighten her shoulders. "You told my father about my job applications. He came to see you and you gave him the information he needed to ruin my chances at being hired on at any of the firms where I'd applied."

Scott looked confused for a moment, then shook his head. "No. I mean, yes. He showed up here and I told him that you weren't coming back, that you were going to find your own way in life. It wasn't so that he could interfere."

"But he did," she said, her voice cracking. "I told you he would. I asked you not to say anything until I had everything settled. He's basically blackballed me in the legal community. I guess I could get in my car and drive to California. That sounds like a great option, right?"

"I didn't—"

"And now you've been reinstated. Do you think that's a coincidence, Scott? According to the conversation I just had with my dad, it isn't. He said he offered you a deal—help limit my options and he'd use his contacts at the Justice Department to have your review abandoned. I guess you both got what you wanted." She drew herself up and asked, "So tell me again, was it worth it?"

"It was a mistake, Lexi." Scott ran his hand through his hair, a gesture so familiar to her now it made pain slice through her once more. "You have to believe that."

"Was it?" she countered. "You've told me over and over how you sabotage your own life. You destroy the connections you have with people."

"Not you—"

"You're a coward." She wanted the words to hurt him. She needed him to feel some of the same pain she did, as if she could hold on to him with any kind of desperate connection.

"Excuse me?" He said the words through clenched teeth.

"I got too close. I think your feelings for me scared the hell out of you and you dealt with them the only way you know how—by pushing me away. Guess what? It worked. I've had a great time, but some things weren't meant to be. I'm not a fighter by nature. I don't want to spend my whole life looking over my shoulder, waiting for the next time my father sticks his nose in my affairs. I'm stronger than I was when I left, and I can go back now, hopefully on my own terms."

She raised her chin, biting down on her lower lip to keep it from trembling. "Tell me I'm wrong." She tried not to let her voice sound as if she was pleading with him. "Tell me there's another way."

For a moment, the pain in his eyes matched her own. He looked as miserable as she felt. She knew that if he reached for her now, told her he loved her and they would figure out another way, she'd believe him. If he could be honest, they might work through this.

But he didn't give her that chance.

He took a step toward her, then stopped. His eyes closed for a second and when he looked at her again, the mask was back in place. The man who cared only about himself had returned. Lexi wondered if he'd ever really left in the first place.

"Don't say I didn't warn you," he told her, his quiet voice a knife across her soul. "I didn't want to hurt you, Lexi, but we both knew it was inevitable. That's the guy I am. It's who I've always been. Maybe you are better back with your father. At least he's an enemy you know."

"And you'll leave Brevia? Leave behind everything you've built here to go back to the Marshals?"

He bit out a harsh laugh. "What have I really done here? I've put a shine on a two-bit bar. Come on, that's no future."

"It's more than that and you know it. It's your family, the friends you've made in this community. Riley's Bar & Grill is a part of the town because of you. You've made a difference. How can you turn your back on that?"

"The town will go on without me. Sam and my dad will do just fine. They were doing fine when I came back into their lives, and it won't take much for things to return to normal."

She wanted to turn and walk away, but something inside her made her keep pushing. "What about you, Scott? What about your pain? Being in Brevia has healed what was broken inside of you. I know that it has."

"When are you going to get it? It's not a piece of me that's damaged. It's the whole thing. I'm broken and there's no fixing it." He paced back and forth in front of her. "I can get on with my life." He stopped, pressed his lips together, then said, "We both can. This was a fun ride while it lasted. You got the adventure you wanted and I had a distraction while I was waiting for things to work out. But it's not real. It never was."

The unexpected rush of sorrow almost brought her to her knees. Wasn't she repeating the same mistakes she'd made with her father? She'd tried to guess what Scott wanted from her. Attempted to meet his expectations without ever knowing what they truly were. She'd hoped their relationship meant something to him, but was too afraid of being rejected to share her feelings. And now when things were difficult, when she wasn't making it easy on him, he shut her out. Just as her dad had done.

She shook her head, not bothering to wipe away the tears that streamed down her face. "It was real for me," she whispered.

Scott's eyes narrowed and she thought he might respond, believed she might have finally found a crack in his armor. But when he said nothing, she finally turned and walked away.

Forever.

The bar was loud and crowded several hours later. It was a Friday night, and in the few short weeks he'd been in Brevia, Riley's Bar had become a favorite hangout for locals and tourists alike. Scott surveyed the room, knowing he should feel pride in what he'd accomplished. All he could see was how he'd ruined things once again.

He poured a round of shots for a group near the front celebrating someone's promotion, then added an extra glass for himself. He hadn't taken a drink of hard liquor since the night he'd moved in with Lexi. The bourbon burned his throat, but nothing could burn away the memory of Lexi's tortured face as he'd watched her heart break in front of him.

It had killed him to see her like that, but he couldn't seem to stop himself from lashing out once she'd accused him of conspiring with her father. Scott was used to people believing the worst about him and meeting their low, low expectations. She'd been different, or so he'd thought. He'd had the crazy idea she'd seen a better side of him, the man he wanted to be. He'd been stupid enough to hope that he could do right by her.

He'd been waiting for her to leave him, but that didn't

make it hurt less. When it was clear he'd once again messed up, he made sure the door shut behind her for good. His whole body felt the loss of her.

Now he had to live with the gaping hole that hours ago had held his heart.

He put down the empty shot glass and noticed Sam standing at the edge of the bar.

"Busy here," Scott shouted, indicating the jumble of people in front of him.

"Make time," Sam replied. "Now."

Scott grabbed the arm of the second bartender. "Max, can you handle this for a few minutes?"

The younger man smiled. "More tips for me."

Scott followed Sam down the back hallway and into his office. He swore Lexi's scent lingered in the air, making him catch his breath.

A half-dozen large garbage bags were piled in front of the desk.

"Your stuff from the apartment," Sam said flatly.

Scott's gut tightened. He hadn't planned on going back there tonight. But to know she'd already packed and shipped him off still got under his skin, even though he knew everything was his fault. As usual. "Is that what you pulled me away for?"

"I know all about making things harder than they need to be," his brother said, instead of answering the question. "I think a Callahan invented the concept. Did you do it on purpose?"

Scott knew Sam was talking about the information he'd given to Lexi's father. "I don't know." He scrubbed his hands across his face. "I was mad and I didn't want to answer the questions he asked. I wanted him gone. I'm not exactly an expert on thinking before I speak.

Lexi is better off without me. Maybe this was the only way to show her that."

"You love her," Sam told him, using his best big-brother voice.

"You don't know anything about me," Scott countered. "You never have. I'm not like you, Sam. I'm the black sheep, the one who messes up. I always have been. Why should this be any different?"

"It's different because you love her. You're different."

"You know what happened, I assume. So you know it's over."

"Do you remember when we were little, before Mom died?"

Scott gritted his teeth. He and Sam rarely talked about their mother's death, about life before that. Hell, they'd had a hard enough time getting through their childhood, with their father gone most of the time. They'd dealt with the pain and loss in different ways. Yet it remained a common bond they shared, pushing them apart while at the same time keeping them tethered to each other.

"You were a fighter, the most stubborn kid ever," Sam told him. "When her drinking got bad, I'd make excuses or try to coddle her through the bad nights."

"You also made a lot of ramen-noodle dinners and sack lunches when she wasn't in any shape to do it herself."

"I tried to gloss it over."

"You were making the best of the situation." Scott closed his eyes for a moment. "I couldn't."

"Not you," Sam agreed. "You'd get in her face, dump the liquor bottles, play games, sing and dance, whatever you could do to keep her engaged with her family.

You made her step up a lot more than she would have otherwise."

"Look where that got all of us. She went out to replace what'd I'd poured down the sink and died because of it."

"She died because she was driving drunk. That wasn't your fault."

"Well, it sure as hell wasn't yours."

"It wasn't any of ours," Sam told him. "Even after that, you kept fighting. Half the reason you got in trouble was to get Dad's attention, to pull him back into our lives."

"It took twenty years for that to happen, and now he's turned into Dr. Phil. I don't think I had anything to do with that."

"Of course you did," his father said from the doorway.

Scott groaned and rolled his eyes in Sam's direction. "Not him, too."

Joe Callahan stepped into room. "Sammy's right. You were a fighter back then. So what happened, son? What made the fight go out of you?"

"The fight didn't go out of me," Scott said through clenched teeth. "If you both remember, I joined the army, I became a marshal. I've spent my whole damn life fighting." He threw out his hands. "Other than these past few weeks. Maybe that's my problem. I'm going soft." He pointed a finger at Sam, then his father. "Just like the two of you. I let this town make me forget my priorities."

Joe came forward, placing his big hands on Scott's shoulders. "This town and that woman gave you priorities. She made you whole."

"She made me think I could be someone I'm not," Scott said quietly. "Lexi and I both learned our lesson there."

"You need to fight for her," Sam countered.

"She doesn't want me to. It's better for both of us if I let her walk away."

"Are you kidding?" His brother slammed his hand down on the desk. "I saw you with her. I know that look. Hell, I avoided that look in the mirror for ages. But I'm telling you that for the rest of your life you'll regret it if you don't try to make this right."

"It's the truth, son." Joe brought his face close to Scott's. "I'm sorry that your mother drove off that night. I'm sorry I left her with no options and that I didn't do right by the two of you after she was gone. I messed us up real good." He drew in a shaky breath.

"Dad, don't cry." Scott's head began to pound. "I don't need this."

"What you need is to have your butt kicked into next week."

Shrugging out of his father's embrace, Scott turned to Sam. "I suppose you're the guy to do it?" His hands curled into fists. He was angry at himself, but if he could take it out on Sam, that worked, too. He wouldn't pass up the opportunity for a decent release of frustration. "Bring it on."

Sam shook his head. "No, thanks. Hitting me isn't going to make you feel any better."

"I think it might." Scott stepped forward. "Because it sure as hell feels wrong that my brother isn't on my side."

"I'm on your side," Sam answered. "Just like you were on mine when you slept with Jenny."

"That's not the same thing."

"I said I'd never thank you, but I am now. Your method was crazy, but you were right. I would have been miserable married to her. If you hadn't shown me her true colors, I might not have come to Brevia. Julia and Charlie might not be a part of my life. Sometimes bad things that happen are for the best in the end."

"And sometimes they aren't. That's how it works with me." Blood thrummed through Scott's head, making it hard to get the words out. "I pushed Mom until she left that night. I should have found a way to convince you that Jenny was the wrong woman. Instead, I took her to bed, making you look like a fool and guaranteeing that you'd cut me out of your life. I didn't confront my partner when I knew he was drinking too much and too often, and he got killed because of it. Try telling his wife and kids that things will work out in the end for them." Scott drew in a ragged breath. "Now I've given Robert Preston the information he needed to make sure Lexi feels like she has no options but to go back to him."

"You aren't responsible for the fate of everyone around you," Joe said sadly. "When are you going to realize that, Scott? You do the best you can and so does everyone else."

"My best is pretty awful, Dad." He turned. "You might be right, Sam. I hate what happened with Lexi and her dad, but it could work out for the best when she moves on with her life and I'm not a part of it."

"That's not what I mean and you know it."

"I'm sorry," Scott said after a long moment. "I want you both to know that."

"You don't need to apologize," his father told him. "We're your family. We love you no matter what."

Scott glanced at Sam. "I bet Julia wants to kill me."

"She'll get over it. Quicker than you will."

"We'll have to see," Scott answered. "I need to get back to the front now."

Joe pulled him close for another hug. To his surprise, Scott felt some comfort in the gesture, but still he shrugged away. "Go home, you two. There's nothing more to be done here."

He walked into the hall, sagging against the wall for a moment before he continued. He was going soft. That must be the reason all of this was hitting him so hard. Normally he could leave his mistakes behind, keep moving so that things didn't catch him. But now he felt weighed down, as if he'd swallowed a load of boulders and was sinking into a deep pool of misery. In a way he welcomed the darkness. It was familiar, and right now Scott clung to that to keep from totally drowning.

He straightened his shoulders and went back to the bar, jumping on top as he put two fingers to his mouth to whistle for the crowd's attention.

"I got some good news today," he shouted, "and everyone here is going to celebrate tonight. This round's on me!"

A loud cheer went up from his customers and he climbed down to a chorus of congratulations and back slaps. The blackness in him expanded until it blotted out all of the light he'd known this past month. He sucked in a breath and forced his mouth into a smile. This was what he knew, and he was going to relearn to live with faking happiness.

Chapter Twelve

"You're running away."

"I was running away when I came to Brevia." Lexi folded another shirt and placed it in the suitcase. "Now I'm going home. That's what most people do after they run away."

"You don't want to go back there." Julia plucked the shirt out of the pile and shoved it back in the drawer as Lexi turned away.

"Quit doing that," she said, shaking her head. "I don't know what I want. Not with the options I have left. I came here to find my independence, and instead I traded being dependent on my father with being dependent on Scott. Those jobs I was looking at—their appeal hinged on keeping me close to D.C. so I could be near him. That was stupid."

"That's love. It makes you do stupid things." Julia shrugged. "Trust me, I know."

"I'm going to be smarter now."

"Smarter isn't going home to be your father's puppet."

"I'm going back on my terms."

"You're going back because that's the easy way out."

"Easy? I've been miserable for the past three days. What part of my swollen face and bags under my eyes looks easy to you?" Lexi growled in her throat as Julia put away another sweater. "Stop unpacking me."

"You don't want to leave. Brevia sucks you in until you're a part of the community. I know you like it here."

"Of course I do," Lexi said miserably. "But what am I supposed to do to make a living? I'm not going back to the bar and...I like being an attorney."

"So be one. In Brevia." Julia pointed a finger at her. "You have a half-dozen clients already. Find some cheap office space and hang out your shingle or whatever it is lawyers do."

"I have a handful of people I've helped on a pro bono basis. I can't be paid with free highlights and apple pies."

"Your hair looks a lot better since Nancy got ahold of you."

Lexi couldn't help but roll her eyes. "Not the point."

"The point is you're afraid to try."

"I did try. And I failed. End of story."

"You didn't really. You told everyone that you were having 'an adventure.' That this was just a short vacation from reality. That's not putting yourself out there for real."

"I left my job, my father, everything I knew behind. How is that not real?"

"You didn't leave them. You said 'I'll be back.' You could be someone different because it was a costume you were trying on. Why bother with the guts to make it work? You knew you could go running home to Daddy."

"Running home…!" Lexi said with a sputter. "I was applying for other jobs. I didn't plan to go back."

Julia shook her head. "I don't believe you."

"How dare you—"

"I don't believe you and I don't think you intended to stay with Scott, either."

"You can't be serious. He's the one who betrayed me."

"He did you a favor."

Lexi felt her mouth drop open. "You're crazy. I don't know why I came here in the first place."

"You came here," Julia answered, "because I'm the only person you know who would let you live your own life. But you can't do it. You're not brave enough. I thought you had it in you, but I guess I was wrong."

"Had what in me?"

"The courage to really stand on your own two feet. Not just take 'a break' from life. Your dad interfered with your job applications. So what? Big deal. Stuff happens. Move on. Apply for more jobs, smaller firms. Start your own firm. Right here. What's stopping you?"

"And what would stop him from interfering again?"

"You will. You're the only one who can stop him. But you have to stand up to him once and for all and be willing to deal with the consequences, no matter what they are. You haven't done that yet. You've told him you 'need time.' To him that's an open door. If you really want to live life on your own terms, you have to force him to let you go."

"That's easier said than done."

"Maybe," Julia agreed. "That's why Scott did you a favor. Eventually your father was going to find out you'd applied for jobs. Did you really have any intention of taking one of them, or was it just a ploy to prove to him you were ready to move on?"

"Yes… No… I don't know, when you say it like that." Lexi sat down on the bed, suddenly tired now that the edge was taken off her anger. "I knew he was going to be mad, but I still haven't proved anything to him. I've shown I can live on my own for a few weeks. So what? I wanted to get a job without his help. Everything I've done in my life has been because my dad has been holding the strings. I went to his alma mater. I worked for his firm on the cases he assigned me. I needed a change. I thought a month would show him that there was more to me than he thought. I wanted to prove it to myself, as well."

"And it did, right?"

"I suppose. But you're right, taking a break and making a fresh start for real are two different things. I'm scared of being alone. I'm afraid to be on my own when it's permanent."

"You're not on your own in Brevia," Julia said softly. "You have friends here. You have Scott."

"I don't." Lexi shook her head. "I have friends and I'm grateful for that. Grateful to you. But I don't have Scott. He's going back to the Marshals. He doesn't want anything long-term with me."

"He loves you," Julia told her. "I can see it."

"I don't think he knows how to let himself love someone." Lexi wiped at her damp eyes with the T-shirt in her hands. "We both knew it was temporary. He made sure of that when he told my father about my plans." She shook her head. "I don't think he did me a favor, but either way, we're done. You're right about one thing, Julia."

"I'm usually right about everything," the other woman corrected with a smile.

Lexi mustered a watery grin in return. "I haven't learned to stand on my own two feet," she said softly. "I didn't take control of my future. I only postponed the future my father has planned for me."

"It's not too late." Julia placed a hand on Lexi's shoulder. "Take it from one who knows, it's never too late. Do you know what you want to do with your life?"

Lexi thought for a minute, then nodded.

"Then go do it."

Lexi took a deep, soul-cleansing breath. "You're right. This isn't over until I say it is." She stood up, then smiled as she looked at the empty suitcase on the bed. "Did you unpack everything?"

Julia shrugged. "I basically threw it all into a drawer, so I'm not saying you'll be able to find what you need. But it's here, Lexi. You belong here."

Lexi nodded. As if the clouds had parted after a heavy storm, her path appeared before her, suddenly clear as a blue sky. "I know what I want. And I know just the person to help me get it."

An hour later, Lexi stood on the steps of Frank Davis's office once again. She raised her hand to knock, but Ida Garvey pushed her aside.

"It's a good thing you called me to meet you. After all, I practically paid for this building," the older woman told her, turning the knob and walking right in. "Frank," she called out. "I know you're hiding out in here."

Frank Davis came forward from the main office. "Ida," he said, his voice dripping with Southern hospitality. "To what do I owe the honor of…" He trailed off when he noticed Lexi standing behind Ida. "Why is she here with you?"

"She's my attorney," Ida said simply.

Lexi couldn't help the smile that curved her lips. Listening to Ida ramble on during the short drive downtown, she'd questioned the logic of including the older woman in this confrontation. But she knew she'd get further with Frank Davis if she had his best client in her corner.

"I'm your attorney," he argued now.

"You were for many years," Ida agreed. "And you did a good job. Mainly. Adequate, anyway. Well, except for that time—"

"What's your point, Ida?" The sweetness had dropped from his tone.

"Something's wrong with you, Frank." Ida pointed a fleshy finger at him. "I don't know what, but I smell trouble on you. You're ignoring clients, messing up filings, generally dropping the ball across the board. I want to know why."

"That's not true." Frank's hand shot up in the air. "It's this…Yankee. She's put these notions into your head."

"Yankee?" Lexi asked. "Did you really just call me that?"

"Hush, girl." Ida turned to Frank. "No one puts any notions into my head and you know it. Spill the beans, Frank."

He puffed himself up as if to argue, then let out his breath in a large burst. Frank Davis sank into the chair behind the secretary's desk and ran a hand across his face. "I'm in love," he said with a loud moan.

Ida looked back at Lexi, a question in her eyes. Lexi

wasn't sure if the question was *Is this guy crazy?* but that was what she was thinking.

"Well, good for you, Frank," Ida said slowly. "Doris has been gone awhile now and the boys are grown and out of the house. You deserve some happiness."

"Happiness," Frank wailed. "There's nothing happy about loving this woman. She torments me every day. Her expectations, her needs. I'll be sixty-three years old next month. There's only so much this old body can handle, even with them little blue pills."

"TMI," Ida said quickly, then, at his odd look, explained, "Too much information, Frank."

"Maybe this was a mistake," Lexi whispered.

Ida ignored her. "Who is this gal?"

A look of pained adoration crossed Frank's ruddy face. "Miss Lucy St. Louis from down in Atlanta."

"Atlanta, Georgia?" Ida asked. "You've taken up with a woman who lives three hours away? Frank, you're a bigger fool than I thought."

"I love her, Ida." Frank dropped his head into his hands. "She loves me, too. But the distance is part of the problem. She wants to see me every weekend, and I've been driving back and forth. Sometimes in the middle of the week, too, if she wants…"

"A booty call?" Lexi couldn't help but ask.

Frank turned red, but mumbled, "She can't get enough."

"Then move her up here." Ida threw her hands in the air. "This isn't rocket science."

"It's not that easy." Frank leaned back in the chair, hands pressed to his temples. "She's got a little sister in private school down there she takes care of, and she makes good money at her job."

"I don't even want to know what someone named Lucy St. Louis does for a living," Ida muttered.

"Probably not," Frank agreed, then sighed. "I'm sorry, Ida. I haven't been giving my clients my all. I'm distracted and tired and..."

"Then why didn't you take my help?" Lexi asked.

"After what you did last year with Julia's son?" Frank shook his head. "I may be an old fool, but I'm not stupid. I don't trust you and I'm sure as hell not entrusting my clients to you."

"I trust her," Ida said firmly. "Lots of other people around town do, as well. Vera Morgan being one of them."

Frank's bug eyes narrowed in on Lexi. "Is that true?"

"It is." Lexi stepped forward. "I want to do right by the people of Brevia, Mr. Davis. Just like you. I know my introduction to the town was poor at best, but I'm a good attorney."

"Can't deny you there," Frank muttered.

"I'd like to stay in town, but I'm not a waitress."

The lawyer raised his head. "I heard you haven't been breaking as many glasses recently."

Lexi bit out a short laugh. "That's true. But I'm a better attorney than the best waitress I could ever be."

"I could use someone working with me," he admitted, scrubbing his hand across his face again. He looked expectantly at Lexi. "I'm going to be retiring here in a few years. If Lucy doesn't kill me first."

Lexi nodded, her mind such a jumble she could barely form a coherent thought. This was really happening. She was going to stay in Brevia. For good.

"It's settled, then," Ida said.

Frank stood and walked around the desk, grabbing

Lexi's hand and shaking it. "Welcome to Davis and Associates." He turned to Ida. "Could you give Lexi and me a few minutes alone to discuss salary and benefits?"

"No way." Ida crossed her arms over her chest. "I'm staying for that part of the conversation."

"You can't leave now."

"It's only for a couple of days." Scott handed Jon Riley a piece of paper. "I've put together a list of deliveries and the schedule for the week with each person's contact information. If you need anything, call my cell phone."

"I'm the cook, not a bar manager," Jon argued, holding the paper tightly.

"You'll do fine." Scott clapped him on the shoulder. "I trust you." *More than I trust myself at this point,* he added silently.

"How can you run away?"

Scott's head began to pound again. "I'm not running away. I have business in D.C."

"Your old job."

He nodded.

"Are you going back to it?"

"I need to discuss some things with them first." Scott rubbed his temples. He wished he was running right now. Away from questions he couldn't answer, away from prying eyes every night at the bar. It had been almost a week since he'd gotten his reinstatement letter, and only three days until the reception for his dad and Sam. Riley's was crowded every night, with many people coming in for dinner and to hang out with friends or family. He'd gotten to know a number of locals, the majority of whom wanted to remind him what a fool he'd been to "fire" Lexi. No matter how many times he explained that she'd quit, the result was the same—everyone telling him how badly he'd messed up.

As if he didn't know that already. He felt the loss of her through every fiber of his being, from the moment he woke up until he dropped to sleep again. His back was killing him from nights on the couch in his office. Sam had offered him a place to stay, and so had his dad, over the objections of both of their wives, he'd guess.

But Scott wasn't going to be a burden to his family, especially not when they were treating him like some fragile doll who'd break in two if not handled the right way. He'd explained over and over that even if he went back to the Marshals, he'd find a good manager for the bar and come back to visit whenever he could. But it didn't seem to be good enough. They wanted him to promise to stay, and he couldn't do that.

He told himself it was because he had too much to lose if he gave up his job, but his heart felt as if he'd already lost everything important when Lexi walked away. Whether he stayed in Brevia or went back to D.C. and the Marshals wasn't really important. All that mattered was that she was gone. His mind might know it was for the best. Hell, he'd almost forced her to leave, but that didn't make it hurt any less. If anything, the ache only intensified, because if he wasn't such a self-destructive fool, he could have prevented it. That part hurt the most.

"You're not leaving, are you?" Misty walked into the kitchen. "Jon says he's going to be in charge now."

Scott rubbed two fingers against his temple. "He isn't in charge. I'm going to D.C. for a few days to wrap up some stuff with my old job."

"Are you coming back?"

He hesitated for the briefest second and she stomped her foot on the floor. "You can't desert us here."

"I'm not deserting anyone," Scott muttered. "I have business to take care of out of town. Jon is going to be running the place for a few days."

"I never agreed to that." Jon slammed the refrigerator door shut.

"The waitresses will never agree to it," Misty repeated. "You'd better make one of them the manager."

Scott wanted to hit something. "Fine. You're in charge."

"I don't want to be the manager," she argued. "Those girls can't get along."

"You two are killing me!"

"We need you, Scott." Misty's voice softened. "I know you don't want to be needed. I know you've been in a terrible mood since Lexi left, but this bar is yours. Like it or not. Take it or leave it."

He saw the expectation in her face, felt it in her tone of voice. It weighed on him, just as it had with Lexi and his family. Why couldn't anyone see that he wasn't a person to depend on? He'd tried to be honest about what he could and couldn't give. It wasn't that hard to understand.

He'd reached his breaking point. This was how it happened with him. People pushed him further than he could manage, always thinking that he'd step up to the challenge. But he never did. As much as he wanted to, he couldn't make it work.

Now was no different.

He grabbed his duffel bag from the floor next to the desk.

"Leave it," he said quietly and walked out the door.

Chapter Thirteen

Lexi heard the fire truck before she saw it. The big red engine came screaming around the corner of Main Street. She stopped midstride walking out of Julia's salon, riveted by the noise of the siren. Then her heart leaped into her throat as the truck pulled up in front of Riley's Bar & Grill.

Scott wasn't there. Julia had told Lexi he'd left town for D.C. Lexi didn't know why the news had shocked her. Even after he'd told her he wasn't going to stick, some part of her had still held out hope. She told herself it didn't matter. It was enough that she'd found a place to call home. If Scott had to keep looking for his happiness, that was no business of hers.

She hadn't been back to the bar since she'd walked out. But she cared about the people there. She'd had lunch with Misty just yesterday, and Jon had stopped by her new office at the end of the day to bring her a take-out dinner. It was concern for her friends that had her running toward the bar, following two firemen inside.

The scene inside stopped her in her tracks. Water gushed through the doorway to the back half of the building. At least two inches covered the floor of the main room, the legs of chairs and tables standing in it.

"Oh, no," she whispered. Jon waded out from the back, a look of pure panic on his face.

"What happened?" she called to him, not wanting to step farther into the wetness.

"Water line broke, I think." He shook his head. "I got here about twenty minutes ago and this is what I found."

"Why is the fire department here?"

"Dave Johnson, a local plumber, is also a volunteer firefighter. I called him first and he brought the truck. I guess they were worried about an electrical fire or something."

A man dressed in a black T-shirt and yellow overalls came up behind Jon. "We've turned off the water. It's going to be tomorrow morning before I can get the parts here to fix it for real."

"What about tonight?" Lexi asked. Thursday was a popular night out in Brevia.

"Unless your customers have rubber boots," Dave told Jon, "they're not going to want to be in the place."

Lexi took off her shoes and rolled up her jeans, sloshing through the water to get to Jon. "Did you call Scott?"

"At least a dozen times," he answered. "He's not taking my calls." The older man shook his head. "With how he tore out of here, I'm not sure he means to come back."

"Of course he's coming back," Lexi answered with

more conviction than she felt. "The reception for Joe and Sam is Saturday night. He's not going to miss that."

"I don't know. He stormed off in quite a huff. Looked to me like he was done with Brevia." Jon shook his head sadly. "Wouldn't surprise me."

A shrill cry had both of them turning toward the door. Misty stood at the entrance. "Did someone forget to turn off a faucet? Why is there a fire engine out front?"

"We have a small situation," Lexi explained. "A water line broke." She turned to Dave Johnson. "What are the options here?"

"Start swimming," he suggested with a smile.

"Not funny."

"Like I said, I'll have the pipe fixed by tomorrow. You're lucky it's fresh water, so that's a plus. Basically, you need to get a team in here to clean things up. I'm guessing it will take a week or so."

Lexi shook her head. "We don't have a week. This place needs to be ready for a party on Saturday night."

"That's right," Dave answered, nodding. "This is the big shindig for Sam Callahan. Sorry, lady, ain't going to happen."

"Who knows what will happen if Scott doesn't get back," Misty called out. "At this point, maybe we should start looking for other work."

"No way," Lexi argued. "We can't leave this place like this. If we don't get this water up quickly, the floor will be ruined. It needs time to dry out. There's got to be something we can do."

"Why do you even care?" Misty asked her. "I thought you were done with this place. Done with Scott Callahan."

"I am done. But I can't let it end like this. Scott poured

his time, energy and money into revitalizing Riley's. I know you all have been making more in tips in the past month than you have in ages."

The waitress nodded slowly.

"We can't just give up on it now."

"What are we supposed to do?" Jon asked.

Lexi turned to Dave. "You said you can get the pipe fixed tomorrow morning?"

"First thing," he promised. "I can make a call to the guys who work on flooded buildings and the like."

"Good." Lexi racked her brain for what to do next. "I'll get ahold of Sam. If anyone can rally the troops around here, it's the police chief."

Jon put a heavy hand on her shoulder. "I'm serious, Lexi. I doubt Scott's coming back. At this point, it might be better to walk away and let him hash things out with the insurance company."

"I don't believe that, Jon." She pointed a finger at him. "He gave you a chance when no one else would, and hired a couple of your buddies for odd jobs around here, right?"

"Yes."

"He's made an investment in Brevia. This place and this town mean something to him. Even if he doesn't realize it yet, he's going to. We have to show him..." Her voice lowered, became shaky. "I have to show him that even if he doesn't believe in himself, I still do. I'm not giving up." She felt her throat tighten with tears. Jon was probably right. For all she knew, Scott wouldn't care what happened here or what she did to make things right. But she had to try. That was what she'd want someone to do for her, and she had to believe her faith would pull him through.

Jon drew her into a tight hug. "You're a good woman, Lexi Preston."

"Let's hope I'm good enough."

Scott thumped his hands on the steering wheel as he drove into town. He'd been calling Jon Riley every fifteen minutes for the past four hours, but Jon hadn't answered his cell. That seemed ominous to Scott, and ominous was the last thing he needed this morning. He'd been delayed an extra night in D.C., wrapping up loose ends. He'd expected to make it to Brevia last evening, but now had only half a day until the reception, and there was so much to do.

If he even had a bar to get back to.

He'd left messages with directions for who to call and how to manage the cleanup. The one time he'd been able to reach Jon, after the man's many messages, their conversation had been cryptic at best. Jon had told him he wouldn't believe what had happened—something about a flood, a miracle, and to return as soon as possible. Then he'd hung up. Scott understood why Jon had been mad. Scott hadn't picked up the phone on Thursday. He'd left his cell in the car while he'd met with his former boss at the U.S. Marshals. That conversation had been bad enough, without having more distractions piled on top.

Now he worried that his carelessness may have put his future in jeopardy once again. It didn't matter, he told himself. He'd get through the reception without letting anyone down. He was going to stick this time. Whatever he found when he got to the bar, he was determined to make it right again.

He came to a screeching halt at the curb and threw his truck into Park. Bolting for the door with his heart in his throat, he rushed through, then stopped, shocked at the scene that awaited him.

The whole bar was decorated in shades of cornflower-blue and lemon-yellow. Linen cloths covered the tables. A mason jar filled with flowers sat in the center of every one. On each corner of the bar was a bouquet of balloons floating into the air. Poster-size photos of his dad and Vera, Sam and Julia, stood on tall easels off to one side. The place looked beautiful and, more importantly, ready for the reception.

"How did this happen?" he whispered, unable to believe how good everything looked. Of all the scenes he could have walked into, this was the last one he'd imagined.

His father was standing inside the front door, surveying the brightly decorated room. "Glad you made it, son." Joe wrapped him in a tight hug. "Did you get everything taken care of in D.C."

Scott nodded numbly. "Where's the water?"

Joe laughed. "You can't very well have a party when people would be getting their feet wet, right?"

"Why didn't anyone pick up when I called?" Scott pulled back from his dad's embrace.

Sam came over and chucked him on the shoulder. "We were kind of busy around here, with your building flooding and all."

"But Lexi had a plan," Misty told him as she finished tying more balloons to the edge of the bar. "She can be quite the mini taskmaster when she sets her mind to it."

"Lexi?" Scott felt his mind go blank.

"She's over at the salon with Julia, Vera and Lainey right now," Sam announced. "Julia insisted that she take a break. Otherwise, she'd still be here working."

He threw his hand out in a sweeping gesture. "All of this is her doing."

"She was convinced something had delayed you in D.C.," Joe explained.

"I went to see Derek's wife. I wanted to explain to her what had happened that day. She needed to hear it from me."

Joe nodded.

"We were ready to give up on you," Misty told him candidly. "Not your dad and brother, I guess. They didn't know about the water damage until Lexi called them. But the other waitresses, Max, Jon—we all thought you'd deserted us and we were ready to return the favor."

"I told you—"

"Everyone knows what you said." Jon came out of the kitchen, an apron tied around his waist. "We also know what you did. You left us behind. You don't have a reputation as someone who sticks. Why would we think this time was any different?"

"Maybe because I told you I'd come back."

"Past actions mean more than words." Jon shrugged. "You should know that."

"But Lexi believed in you," Misty told him. "Even when the rest of us didn't have faith, she never actually gave up on you." The waitress clasped him in a quick hug. "Who knew she'd be right?"

"Are you here for the party or to stay?" Sam asked quietly.

Scott hesitated, his mind a whir. For the first time in as long as he could remember, he didn't feel alone. Someone had his back. He'd done his best to push Lexi away, but she'd stayed true. Even though he didn't deserve it.

He was going to change that. If this time had taught him anything, it was that he didn't have to be a prisoner to his own doubts and fear. He could make things right and he had every intention of doing that.

Starting now.

Chapter Fourteen

Her nails drying, Lexi tried to feign interest in the latest magazine gossip. Her eyes drifted shut as she listened to Julia, Lainey and Vera talk, and wondered what it would be like to have grown up with sisters and a mother. The easy camaraderie and obvious closeness was something she'd never experienced. But she'd learned there was no use wishing for things that couldn't be. That might have been the biggest lesson from her grand adventure this past month.

She'd spent her whole life trying to make the people around her happy. Her only goal had been to live up to everyone's perfect image. Each time, the expectations had changed, when she got near enough to believe she might actually accomplish what she'd set out to do.

Now she knew she could only do her best and keep moving forward. She had to be true to herself and what she knew was right. That was what she'd told her father last night on the phone when she'd explained that she wasn't coming back to Ohio. He'd yelled and threatened, and although she'd been shaking with emotion, she'd held steady to her path. Eventually, he'd calmed down, and although he hadn't liked what she was saying, she'd gotten him to agree to stop interfering in her new life. She'd invited him to visit, offered him a chance to get to know her as her own person. He hadn't accepted, but hadn't outright refused, either.

She'd also done all she could for tonight's reception. Part of it was for Julia and Vera. They'd taken her into their circle even though she'd once tried to rip apart their family. They accepted her for who she was now and helped her gain the confidence to believe in herself. No one had given her a second chance like that before.

It taught her a great deal about how to live. Her heart still ached every day for Scott, but her belief in him had been a big part of why she'd stepped up to the plate. She knew that no one had ever given him a second chance when he needed it. That might have been because he'd never stuck around long enough to earn it. But it didn't matter. She believed in him, in who he was deep in his soul. She'd caught glimpses of the tender, honorable man he was inside. Yes, that man was buried under layers of pain and fear, but he was still the essence of who Scott was.

Even if he didn't come back for the reception, she knew he'd eventually talk to Joe or Sam. She wanted Scott to know that he could count on her when it mattered most. Because to her that was what love was, and even if he couldn't return her feelings, that didn't lessen what she felt for him.

A hush fell over the salon and she opened her eyes, wondering what had caught everyone's attention. Scott Callahan stood in the doorway, looking tired, beautiful and directly at her.

Julia strode forward at the same time Lexi rose to her feet, as if something in him pulled her closer.

"You've got a lot of nerve coming here," his sister-in-law told him, her finger wagging. "After—"

"I know," he said, holding up a hand, his eyes never leaving Lexi's. "I'm sorry and you can lay into me later. I need a few minutes to talk to Lexi."

To her surprise, Julia stepped back to let him pass.

Lexi felt her breath begin to come out in short, nervous puffs of air. "I wasn't sure you were coming back."

He nodded. "It may be the first non-idiot move I've made in the past couple of weeks. I'm sorry, Lexi."

He was standing in front of her now, so close she could see that he needed a shave. She could pick out the bright flecks of gold in his blue eyes. She could feel the warmth radiating from him, smell his soap and minty gum. Her whole body tingled, as if telling her how badly it had missed him.

"You hurt me. A lot."

"It won't happen again," he whispered. "I promise."

She glanced around at all the women staring at them and knew that she'd remember this moment, no matter how it ended, for the rest of her life.

"I'm staying in Brevia. I talked to my father and told him he can't run my life anymore."

"I talked to him, too."

Her heart sank. "To thank him for getting your job back?"

"To tell him I wasn't going back to the Marshals. That

even if he wanted to make the lies he told true, there was nothing he could offer to make me betray you again."

Lexi's mouth dropped. She didn't know how to answer.

"You're not going back?" she finally asked.

"I want to make my life in Brevia, Lexi." His eyes looked hopeful. "With you, if you'll have me again. I know I pushed you away. I broke your trust and it kills me that I hurt you."

He reached forward and laced his fingers in hers. "I'm nothing without you. You make me the person I was meant to be. I want to spend our whole lives together."

"What about action and adventure? What about adrenaline and the thrill of the chase?"

"Building our life together is all the adventure I need." He raised her fingers to his lips and kissed the tip of each one. "Every time I look at you is a bigger rush than anything else I could imagine. I want to let you into every part of my life. I want to know all there is to know about you. Good and bad. I love you, Lexi. With everything I am and everything I have. Give me a chance to prove it to you."

She heard several women sigh. "If you don't take him back, I'm coming after him," one lady said from underneath a dryer.

A smile broke across Lexi's face. "Oh, I'm taking him. He's officially off the market," she whispered and threw her arms around his neck.

Scott kissed her deeply, holding her tight against him for several minutes.

Then Julia moved closer. "Do I get to kick your butt now?" she asked him.

Lexi laughed. "Do you still want to?"

Julia hesitated, then smiled. "I guess I'll give you a pass. Since you're family and that was a pretty good speech."

Scott looked at Lexi. "I meant every word of it." He took a step away from her. "But there's one more thing."

Lexi's eyes widened as he dropped to one knee.

"Lexi Preston," he said, pulling a small box from his jacket pocket, "will you marry me? I want to know you're mine forever."

"Yes," she breathed, and he slipped a perfect pear-shaped diamond onto her finger. "Yes, yes, yes."

She looked at him and knew the happiness she saw in his eyes was reflected in her own. He stood, pulling her close once again. Then he looked over his shoulder at Julia and Vera, both of whom were wiping at their eyes.

"Could we expand tonight's celebration to include an engagement?"

"That's a perfect idea," Vera said, and Julia nodded.

Scott turned back to Lexi. "What do you think? Do you mind going public so soon?"

She nodded in turn, happiness filling her completely. "I think all three Callahan men have finally found a place to call home."

Epilogue

"Who wants pie?"

Vera Morgan Callahan came into the dining room with Joe following her, a pie plate in each hand.

"Me do," Charlie shouted from his seat at the end of the table.

Lexi smiled as Julia ruffled his hair. "Are you sure, buddy?" his mom asked. "You practically ate your weight in mashed potatoes."

Charlie grinned at her. "Want more pie and more taters."

Sam laughed. "You get your healthy appetite from your uncle Scott. As a kid, he could put away more food on Thanksgiving than anyone has a right to without puking."

"You eat pie, too." Charlie pointed a chubby finger at Scott.

Scott stretched an arm across the back of Lexi's chair, fingers tickling her shoulder. "You betcha, Charlie. Let's have a couple of pieces and head out back. I want to show you how to throw a football the right way."

"Like I haven't already?" Sam tried to look offended, but his big grin ruined the effect.

Ethan cleared his throat from his seat across the table. "Did you forget you have a real-life former quarterback in the room?"

"You want to prove you've still got your skills in a friendly game?" Scott asked.

Ethan smiled in return. "I've got my hands full here." He glanced down at the baby sleeping in his arms and dropped a kiss on the top of his daughter's head.

Ruby's adoption had been finalized a month ago, and Ethan and Lainey had brought her home. Ruby was a chunky cherub of a baby, sweet and smiley. Lexi knew they'd had a long road to finally have their own baby. It was clear that Ruby completed their family, and everyone in the whole town seemed to dote on her, including Scott.

His eyes softened and he gave Lexi's arm a little squeeze. "That's a good excuse, Daniels." He leaned close to Lexi's ear and whispered, "I can't wait until I have one of my own."

His voice sent a quick shiver down her spine. He kissed the side of her neck and the shivers traveled south. They'd been married only a couple months and weren't even trying for babies yet. Scott was busy with the bar and Lexi was building her practice and taking on more clients as Frank transitioned to more part-time work. But they were certainly practicing, as Scott called it, quite a bit. He joked that he wanted to get it right when they were finally ready. And there was no arguing that he got it very right.

"Lainey, take that baby from your husband." Julia stood and picked up her plate. "I'm either going to suffocate from all the testosterone in the air or lose my tasty turkey watching the newlyweds over here." She waved her hand in the direction of the backyard. "You boys take it outside while we clean up. You can have pie later."

Sam reached for her plate. "You should go sit down, Juls. I'll help with the dishes. In your condition—"

"I'm pregnant. I can still carry plates."

He placed a protective hand on her round belly. "I don't want you to get worn down."

She kissed his cheek. "You didn't seem too worried last night."

Ethan groaned and pushed back from the table. "Enough already." He transferred Ruby to Lainey's arms. "Joe, do you think you can help me whip your sons?"

"Absolutely." Joe turned to Vera. "Mind if we postpone dessert?"

"Go for it." She took the pies from his hands and set them on the table. "Just take it easy on these boys. Even though they're younger, I doubt they have your stamina."

Joe wrapped her in one of his trademark hugs. "Only for you, sweetheart."

Scott made a face. "That's my cue to get out of here." Lexi giggled as he scrambled from his seat.

Sam helped Charlie climb out of the high chair and the three other men followed them toward the backyard.

"I'm happy to clean up the dishes," Lexi said, collecting plates and glasses. "You three can have a seat."

"Look at you, putting your month as a bar wench to good use," Julia teased.

Vera shook her head. "You don't have to do it by yourself." She waved her hands at her two daughters, clearly shooing them away. "You girls take Ruby to the living room. Lexi and I will take care of this."

A grin broke across Lainey's face. "Do you hear that, Ruby honey? Not only are you the best baby in the whole wide world, but now you've earned me a hall pass from kitchen duty."

"Don't just stand there." Julia scurried around the table. "Let's get out of here before she changes her mind."

As the two sisters disappeared through the doorway, Lexi turned to Vera. "I'm fine to take care of this on my own. It's the least I can do." She felt emotion rise in her throat and swallowed it down. "This is the best Thanksgiving I've ever had."

"I'm a decent cook," Vera agreed, "but not that good."

Lexi shook her head. "The meal was amazing, but it's everything about it. It's having all of you around me, feeling like I'm part of a family. I can't tell you how much I appreciate it."

"I don't mind the cleanup," Vera said as she picked up several plates and led Lexi into the kitchen. "If you haven't noticed, I'm a bit of a control freak." She laughed when Lexi didn't respond and began stacking plates in the dishwasher. "I'm sorry your father couldn't make it down."

Lexi sighed. "Me, too, but he's still having trouble adjusting to me living my own life. I'm glad he came to the wedding, and he promised to fly down for a few days over Christmas." She picked up a casserole pan and dunked it into the sink filled with hot, soapy water. "We're taking small steps, which is more than I ever thought I'd get from him."

"And you're happy still?" Vera asked quietly.

"So happy. I couldn't imagine anyplace feeling more like home than Brevia." She rinsed the pan with clean water and lifted it out of the sink. "I feel lucky to have all of you in my life, especially Scott."

"I'm the lucky one."

Lexi felt Scott's arms wrap around her waist. He took the pan from her hands and stepped to her side. "I'll dry."

"How are the boys doing out there?" Vera asked.

"Charlie's scored two touchdowns. We may have a future football star on our hands."

Vera smiled. "I have to see that. Can you two handle the rest of this mess?"

"Absolutely," Lexi answered. "We're almost finished, anyway." She loaded the last of the glasses into the dishwasher as Vera disappeared into the backyard.

Lexi straightened, to find Scott watching her, his gaze warming her from the inside out. He held out his hand and she stepped into his arms, his familiar scent still making her heart dance as he pulled her close. "I love you," she whispered.

His lips brushed against her forehead. "You are everything to me. You're my home, my heart, my whole life. I love you, Lexi. Everything about you, who you are…who I am when I'm with you. I can't imagine anything better than where we are right now."

His words filled her soul, though Lexi couldn't help but laugh. "In Vera's kitchen?"

"In a kitchen, a dining room. Standing in the middle of the street. It doesn't matter as long as we're together."

"Always." She brought her mouth to his, sealing the promise with a kiss.

* * * * *

COMING NEXT MONTH FROM

HARLEQUIN

SPECIAL EDITION

Available June 19, 2014

#2341 MILLION-DOLLAR MAVERICK
Montana Mavericks: 20 Years in the Saddle! • by Christine Rimmer

Cowboy Nate Crawford epitomizes the phrase "new money." He secretly just won millions in the lottery, and he can't wait to cash out and leave Rust Creek Falls. But then Nate meets gorgeous nurse Callie Kennedy, who doesn't give a flying Stetson about money, and all he's ever dreamed of might be in the home he wants to leave behind....

#2342 DATING FOR TWO
Matchmaking Mamas • by Marie Ferrarella

Erin O'Brien is too busy bringing her toy company to new heights to play house with just any man. But speaking at a local Career Day might lead to a whole new job—mommy! When she meets hunky lawyer Steve Kendall and his son, Erin can't help but fall for the adorable twosome. Will Erin be the missing piece in their family puzzle?

#2343 THE BACHELOR'S BRIGHTON VALLEY BRIDE
Return to Brighton Valley • by Judy Duarte

Clayton Jenkins is going undercover...in his own business. The tech whiz wants to find out why his flagship store is failing, so he disguises himself as an employee and gets to work. But even a genius can't program every step of his life—like falling for single mom Megan Adams and her young children! What's a billionaire to do?

#2344 READY, SET, I DO!
Rx for Love • by Cindy Kirk

Workaholic Winn Ferris receives the surprise of his life when he gets custody of an eight-year-old boy. He enlists neighbor Hailey Randall to help him with the child, but Winn can't help but marvel at the bubbly speech therapist. She might just be the one to lift the businessman's nose from the grindstone to gaze into her beautiful baby blues—and fall in love....

#2345 A BRIDE BY SUMMER
Round-the-Clock Brides • by Sandra Steffen

Apple orchard owner Reed Sullivan is frantic with worry when a baby appears on his doorstep. Did his one-night stand from a year ago yield a (too) fruitful crop? So Reid's blindsided when a radiant redhead rescues him from a car accident. Ruby O'Toole has sworn off men, but the quirky bar owner might have it bad for the man she saved—and his insta-family!

#2346 A DOCTOR FOR KEEPS
by Lynne Marshall

Desdemona "Desi" Rask shows up on her grandmother's doorstep to learn about her family in the town of Heartlandia. But Fate throws a wrench in her plans when she meets Dr. Kent Larson and his adorable son. As Desi discovers more about her relatives, she wonders: Can she have a future with Kent, or will her past keep them apart forever?

YOU CAN FIND MORE INFORMATION ON UPCOMING HARLEQUIN® TITLES, FREE EXCERPTS AND MORE AT WWW.HARLEQUIN.COM.

HSECNM0614

SPECIAL EXCERPT FROM

⬥ HARLEQUIN®

SPECIAL EDITION

Enjoy this sneak preview of
DATING FOR TWO
by USA TODAY bestselling author Marie Ferrarella!

***

"Well, you'll be keeping your word to them—I'll be the one doing the cooking."

One of the things he'd picked up on during his brief venture into the dating realm was that most professional women had no time—or desire—to learn how to cook. He'd just naturally assumed that Erin was like the rest in that respect.

"Didn't you say that you were too busy trying to catch up on everything you'd missed out on doing because you were in the hospital?"

"Yes, and cooking was one of those things." She laughed. "A creative person has to have more than one outlet in order to feel fulfilled and on top of their game. Me, I come up with some of my best ideas cooking. Cooking relaxes me," she explained.

"Funny, it has just the opposite effect on me," he said.

"Your strengths obviously lie in other directions," she countered.

Steve had to admit he appreciated the way she tried to spare his ego.

He watched Erin as she practically whirled through his kitchen, getting unlikely ingredients out of his pantry and his cupboard. She assembled everything on the counter within easy reach, then really got busy as she began making dinner.

He had never been one who enjoyed being kept in the dark. "If you don't mind my asking, exactly what do you plan on making?"

"A frittata," she said cheerfully. Combining a total of eight eggs in a large bowl, she tossed in a dash of salt and pepper before going on to add two packages of the frozen mixed vegetables. She would have preferred to use fresh vegetables, but beggars couldn't afford to be choosers.

"A what?"

In another pan, she'd quickly diced up some of the ham she'd found as well as a few slices of cheddar cheese from the same lower bin drawer in the refrigerator.

She was about to repeat the word, then realized that it wasn't that Steve hadn't heard her—the problem was that he didn't know what she was referring to.

Opening the pantry again, she searched for a container of herbs or spices. There were none. She pushed on anyway, adding everything into the bowl with the eggs.

"Just think of it as an upgraded omelet. You have ham and bread," she said, pleased.

"That's because I also know how to make a sandwich without setting off the smoke alarm," he told her.

"There is hope for you yet," she declared with a laugh.

Watching her move around his kitchen as if she belonged there, he was beginning to think the same thing himself—but for a very different reason.

***

Don't miss DATING FOR TWO,
coming July 2014 from Harlequin® Special Edition.

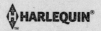

SPECIAL EDITION

Life, Love and Family

Coming in July 2014

THE BACHELOR'S BRIGHTON VALLEY BRIDE

by *USA TODAY* bestselling author

Judy Duarte

Clayton Jenkins is going undercover...in his own business. The tech whiz wants to find out why his flagship store is failing, so he disguises himself as an employee and gets to work. But even a genius can't program every step of his life—like falling for single mom Megan Adams and her young daughter! What's a billionaire to do?

Don't miss the latest edition of the
Return to Brighton Valley miniseries!

*Look for **THE DADDY SECRET**,
already available from the **Return to Brighton Valley**
miniseries by Judy Duarte!*

Available wherever books and ebooks are sold!

Love the Harlequin book
you just read?

Your opinion matters.

Review this book on your favorite
book site, review site, blog or your own
social media properties and share
your opinion with other readers!

HARLEQUIN®

A *Romance* FOR EVERY MOOD™

**Stay up-to-date on all your
romance-reading news with the
Harlequin Shopping Guide,
featuring bestselling authors, exciting new
miniseries, books to watch and more!**

The newest issue will be delivered right to you
with our compliments! There are 4 each year.

Signing up is easy.

EMAIL

ShoppingGuide@Harlequin.ca

WRITE TO US

HARLEQUIN BOOKS
Attention: Customer Service Department
P.O. Box 9057, Buffalo, NY 14269-9057

OR PHONE

1-800-873-8635 in the United States
1-888-343-9777 in Canada

Please allow 4-6 weeks for delivery of the first issue by mail.